OVERNIGHT SERVICE

LAUREN BLAKELY

ALSO BY LAUREN BLAKELY

Big Rock Series

Big Rock

Mister O

Well Hung

Full Package

Joy Ride

Hard Wood

One Love Series

The Sexy One

The Only One

The Hot One

The Knocked Up Plan

Come As You Are

The Heartbreakers Series

Once Upon a Real Good Time

Once Upon a Sure Thing

Once Upon a Wild Fling

Sports Romance

Most Valuable Playboy

Most Likely to Score

Lucky In Love Series

Best Laid Plans

The Feel Good Factor

Nobody Does It Better

Unzipped

Always Satisfied Series

Satisfaction Guaranteed

Instant Gratification

Overnight Service

Never Have I Ever

Special Delivery

The Gift Series

The Engagement Gift

The Virgin Gift (coming soon)

The Exclusive Gift (coming soon)

The Sexy Suit Series

Lucky Suit

Birthday Suit

From Paris With Love

Wanderlust

Part-Time Lover

Standalones

Stud Finder

The V Card

The Real Deal

Unbreak My Heart

The Break-Up Album

21 Stolen Kisses

Out of Bounds

The Dating Proposal

The Caught Up in Love Series

Caught Up In Us

Pretending He's Mine

Playing With Her Heart

Stars In Their Eyes Duet

My Charming Rival

My Sexy Rival

The No Regrets Series

The Thrill of It

The Start of Us

Every Second With You

The Seductive Nights Series

First Night (Julia and Clay, prequel novella)

Night After Night (Julia and Clay, book one)

After This Night (Julia and Clay, book two)

One More Night (Julia and Clay, book three)

A Wildly Seductive Night (Julia and Clay novella, book 3.5)

The Joy Delivered Duet

Nights With Him (A standalone novel about Michelle and Jack)

Forbidden Nights (A standalone novel about Nate and Casey)

The Sinful Nights Series

Sweet Sinful Nights

Sinful Desire

Sinful Longing

Sinful Love

The Fighting Fire Series

Burn For Me (Smith and Jamie)

Melt for Him (Megan and Becker)

Consumed By You (Travis and Cara)

The Jewel Series

A two-book sexy contemporary romance series

The Sapphire Affair

The Sapphire Heist

ABOUT

Top three reasons why sleeping with the enemy is a bad idea...

1. She's my fiercest rival.

2. She's also my firey ex.

3. We're going up against each other in a stiff competition to win the hottest new client on the market.

And yet, I'd like to be up against the wall in a stiff competition to get her to call out my name.

Time to double down on my resistance to her tough-as-nails, take-no-prisoners, sexy-as-sin attitude. The same attitude I find irresistible.

That's a big problem, because in this race to nab the client, I run into Haven in the hotel, on the beach, in the guest quarters late at night.

Hate sex would be a terrible idea.

Except, it's the complete opposite, and now we can't keep our hands off each other.

Trouble is, I'm not so sure it's hate I'm feeling anymore.

And that's the biggest reason sleeping with the enemy you're falling for is a bad idea — my job literally depends on never letting her into my heart.

OVERNIGHT SERVICE

by Lauren Blakely

PROLOGUE

Josh

Show of hands: sleeping with the enemy—good idea or bad idea?

Wait. Don't answer that.

I know it's a motherfucking terrible idea.

As in, shut it down, zip it up, turn around, and run.

Do not pass Go, just *run as fast as you can.*

Why?

Because enemies are enemies for a reason. For *all* the reasons.

But remembering that can be challenging.

Especially when some enemies are so damn good at tricking you into bending rules until they break one night in her hotel room.

Fine, fine. Maybe going to her room was my first mistake if I wanted to keep her far away.

And I absolutely do.

I *have* to.

That's why I've laid down a new set of rules for this one foe in particular.

One gorgeous, brilliant, too-seductive-for-my-own-good archenemy.

This is how it needs to be:

Don't be distracted by her sassy, fiery mouth.

Don't get waylaid by her sexy-as-sin attitude.

And definitely don't lose your focus over that absolutely alluring voice; tight, toned body; or long, lush hair.

Enemies can wear all sorts of faces. Mine is disguised as the woman I'm most attracted to in . . . oh, say, the entire fucking universe.

That's real helpful.

I need autoplay in my brain to remind me: she's stolen clients, she's stolen business, and the woman has tried—oh hell, did she ever try—to steal my heart.

But *that*? I won't let *that* happen.

No way.

No how.

Never.

She's not only the enemy. She's my toughest competition and my fiercest rival. That means I won't give in again. I can't give in another time.

I've got the arsenal to resist her. My strategies are finely tested, my approach sharpened. I don't budge an inch. I don't play nice. And I don't let her know how she affects me.

I am iron around her.

Now, a potential client throws out the playbook, and I have to devise a whole new strategy. Because it looks like I'll be eating, sleeping, and breathing the same goddamn air as the enemy for the next week.

All I have to do is keep my eye on the prize.

And I do, until the night the game changes.

1

JOSH

There's a first time for everything.

Today, it's for tassels.

I am wearing tassels and rocking a look a few buddies picked out for me: long, golden hair; a luau skirt; and the tassels strategically attached to seashells . . . on my chest.

Fine. It's a bra. Okay? I'm wearing a seashell bra.

And I'm owning it as I stride down the concourse at Yankee Stadium, along the third baseline. Not going to lie—I'm getting a lot of looks.

Not the New York seen-it-all-before glance, but the whip-the-head-around, is-he-really-wearing-*that* gawk.

"The votes are in, and it's unanimous—I am undeniably delectable," I say to Ford and Viviana, the assholes responsible for picking my clothes. If you can even call this attire *clothes*. More like strings and doodads.

Viviana slides into full-on faux fashionista mode, setting a long, manicured fingernail against her lips and sidebarring to her husband. "He's definitely wearing it well, but it's sooooo 2016, now that I see the ensemble in person. Maybe he needs to wear strappy sandals instead of those flip-flops. What do you think?"

Ford shakes his head. "No way, honey bunny. This getup—a trend I'm going to call 'embarrass the hell out of your friend'—is always in fashion."

I hold out my arms, turning in a circle outside a memorabilia stand peddling signed jerseys. "He's right. You can never go wrong with 'the dickheads at my office dressed me up' look."

Viviana clasps a hand to her chest. "Aww. You called me a dickhead. I'm so honored."

"You've always been a dickhead, Viv," I say.

Ford arches a brow. "That's my woman you're talking smack about."

"*Your* woman who *I* introduced you to. So I believe you meant to say, 'That's my woman you're talking smack about, and thank you for the millionth time for hooking me up with the love of my life.'"

Ford seems to consider this for a moment as we wind our way past a pretzel vendor. "True. I do owe you."

Viviana nudges him. "But today, Josh owes us." She turns to me, her green eyes chiding. "You are seriously the worst at bets."

I shrug, hakuna-matata style. "And I have zero

complaints," I say as we scan the stadium's aisle numbers, finding our section. Per the rules of today's hula-girl-meets-a-mermaid look, I bought tickets like a civilian for this game, though I could easily have pretty much any box seat in the house. But the purpose of the bet was to have as many people as possible witness my public embarrassment here at the Yankees' first game against the Red Sox this season.

Viviana rubs her palms together then flicks her blonde ponytail off her shoulder. "Maybe we can get the Jumbotron to capture a shot of Josh looking so stylish and sexy."

Ford's eyes light up. "Yes, let's go make a deal with the board operator right now."

I tilt my head in an "aw shucks, guys" false modesty, clasp my hands over my seashell covered heart, and gush, "Aww. You guys are so sweet, trying to embarrass me in front of fifty thousand people. But nothing can get me down today. Not even a shot of *moi* up on the screen looking fabulous."

"Then," Ford says importantly, stopping in his tracks at the steps and motioning to his wife, "you deserve all eyes on you." Ford spins in a circle, cups his hands in a megaphone around his mouth, and shouts, "This man is the man! Just look at him. He is a badass in the negotiation room, even in a clamshell brassiere."

A guy in glasses strolls by, scratches his chin, and says, "What bet did you lose?"

I smile. "Exactly. Thank you. Clearly you understand the ways of the world."

That's the only reason I would show up at the ballpark looking like it's Halloween night at a frat house. Nothing against dudes who dress in drag. To each his own bra and wig. But . . . time and place, you know.

This time, I lost a wager with these guys, my fellow agents.

"All right, hula mermaid girl, time to get us beers," Viviana says.

"Beers too? As well as all this?" I gesture to the outlandish getup and the seats we're sitting in.

"Don't try to get out of it now, Summers," Ford says. "A bet is a bet."

"And it's all worth it, thanks to that glorious bonus clause my client activated when he was World Series MVP." I stroke my chin like I'm lost in a fond memory.

Viv lifts a finger. "Which led to a glorious book deal," says the shark of a literary agent, who works at our firm on the publishing side. She blows on her red fingernails. "I love multiple zeroes."

"I love multiples of nearly everything," Ford chimes in.

"And, yes, I will buy the beers as promised, and in fact, I'll buy beers for the whole section at the end of the first inning," I add.

Ford thrusts his arms in the air, whooping for the hundreds who have just become my temporary best friends. "Free beer. I'll do anything for free beer."

Viv furrows her brow. "Let's define 'anything.' Because you haven't mowed the yard in . . . oh, say, forever. Will you mow the lawn for free beer? Or do you actually want me to hire a hot lawn boy?"

Ford growls, and I swear steam billows from the top of his skull. "You are not hiring a hot lawn boy."

I cup my hand over the side of my mouth, whispering to his wife, "Now we know his weak spot. The fear of the lawn boy. Just imagine if you had horses, Viv. You could hint at hiring a hot stable guy."

"I've always seen myself as the kind of woman who'd have a menagerie of hot boys—stable boy, pool boy, lawn boy . . ."

Ford shoos me off. "Go. I need to have a chat with my woman about this hot-lawn-boy threat."

"Rather than chat, it seems like maybe you ought to mow the lawn," I tell him. "Just an idea though."

"And if you don't," Viviana says to Ford, "I promise I'll only hire a lawn boy who's younger and better looking than you. Fair deal, right?" she asks.

His eyes narrow to slits. "Woman, I am going to put you over my lap and spank you tonight."

"You say that like it's a threat," she says.

I cover my ears. "Get a room, get a room." I point in the direction of the beer stall that sells the good stuff—craft beer, since I am a certified beer snob. "And on that note, I will fetch your beers, dickheads." To the stands, I say, "And I'll cover everyone else's here when the beer guy comes around."

I leave to a chorus of "Love you, man" and "You're the best" and "You can wear that skirt anytime."

I head toward Lana's Beer Den, a bar behind home plate that sells excellent pale ales. It's new, but a guy I know who runs a beer podcast recommended the place, and he wasn't wrong.

Once more, I draw a lot of side-eyes, double takes, and whispers on my way.

And I do not care. Because my colleagues and I all benefited from the Yankees winning the World Series last year and we're celebrating now.

Even several months later, I'm still riding that World Series high, especially here in the stadium. I happily run the mental tape of the last five minutes of that game as I head along the concourse to the beer stand and get in line. The sun beats down on my shoulders, and I lower my shades over my eyes, savoring the moment.

Life is grand.

"Wow, I had no idea you'd look so good in a skirt."

I close my eyes, groaning privately, wishing I wasn't hearing the sexiest voice in the entire universe. But I'd recognize it anywhere. Especially at a ballpark, because this is her stomping ground as much as it's mine.

Haven Delilah.

My former colleague. My former protégé. And my former lover.

Now, my fiercest rival.

I turn around, bracing myself to remain immune to the chestnut hair, the deep brown eyes, the legs for days.

And the freckles, dear God, the adorable fucking freckles on the face of America's sweetheart. That's what the sports reporters dubbed her more than a decade ago when the American-born, French Alps–raised athlete won gold at age twenty-one, snowboarding for the US in the Olympics.

She's the woman who haunts my dirty dreams uninvited, and that is the worst kind of *Inception*-level shit, as far as I'm concerned.

Now here she is at the beer stand at Yankee Stadium, looking as sexy as she had every day at the office in her zip-up dresses and skirts. There is little hotter on a woman than those form-fitting skirts with exposed zippers that make you want to unzip them. All. Day. Long.

Athletic clothes look good on her too.

And so, I'm learning now, do jeans and a T-shirt.

"But you know I have fantastic legs," I say.

"You think I actually remember what your legs look like?" she tosses back, gesturing derisively to my legs.

I don't take the bait. "No time like the present to get reacquainted, then. Here they are, in all their glory."

"Hairy glory."

"Would you prefer I shave?"

She taps her chin and casts her gaze heavenward, her full, glossy pink lips looking entirely kissable. "That would imply that I actually care what you do."

"And yet, you were the one checking out how I look in a skirt."

She heaves a sigh, takes a sip of her beer, then shoots me a steely stare. "Summers, you're parading around a major league ballpark wearing a luau skirt with seashells affixed to your pecs. It's not that I'm checking you out. It's that you're putting on a show. And I find the show . . . Hmm, what's the right word?" She pauses, deliberates, and eyes me up and down. "*Amusing.*"

It's the way she says that last word that makes it a sly insult. I'm *amusing*, as if she wants to pat me on the head, pick me up, maybe put me in her pocket.

"What can I say? If I'm going to dress up for a long homestretch against the enemy, I might as well amuse people."

"Is that what you're doing? Not moonlighting as a hula-girl mermaid with a wig? Is that a thing?" She arches one brow, her tone just as fiery as I'd expect from the woman who believes I'm the reason she lost her job.

She's not entirely wrong.

But she's not right either.

I glance down at my skirt, fingering a grass strand. "You think anyone would hire me? Because maybe I could get some cash on the side."

A smirk seems to tug at her lips. "Think of all the

great drag bars in the city who'd be interested. I can picture you in some kinky boots. Could you get those red ones that go all the way up your legs?" she asks, bending over and dragging her hands up her legs.

Oh, hell. Why did she have to demonstrate? Because . . . that look, that position, the curve of her breasts. *Her.*

I shake off the image I just enjoyed. "I'll take that under advisement. But really, you're welcome to stare all you want. In fact, I highly encourage you to."

I step to the side, swaying, and raise my arms. I even hum a little as I give her my best hula dance.

She rolls her eyes. Her gorgeous chocolate-brown eyes. "It's funny that you think I'm looking at you for any reason other than entertainment."

"It *was* wildly entertaining when Lorenzo capped off an epic World Series with the MVP trophy. That's why I'm wearing this—I underestimated the number of runs for the game, so when he overdelivered, I had to make good on a bet with my colleagues."

"Ah, so you're a betting man."

"I am indeed."

She steps closer, takes a drink of her beer, and lets her eyes tour my body once more. "If you want to bet again, you ought to go up against me. I'm a fierce competitor."

"What a shock."

She shrugs nonchalantly. "I only suggest it because I play hard and I bet hard, and it seems maybe you like to lose."

I puff out my chest, the seashells on my pecs probably not doing me any favors, but hell if this woman would ever grant me a favor. "No regrets on this loss. It activated a shit-ton of bonuses for my guy. The same guy you were going after last year too. But I got him."

She pats my shoulder. "It's so lovely when you remind me that your dick is bigger than mine."

"You know exactly how big it is."

Her eyes darken, blazing with a fiery sort of indignation. "Not as big as your ego. But way to go, trotting out your clients' accomplishments. Why don't you name-drop some more?"

I grit my teeth, hating that she's onto something. That maybe I do come across as a cocky asshole around her. But if the shoe fits . . . "I could, but I don't think you have all day to hear about the megadeals for the superstars I rep."

Those eyes? Forget blazing. There's a five-alarm fire of *rage-hate* crackling in her irises now. But then she turns the ire down to a simmer, waving a hand dismissively. "So many fading names. Maybe someday you'll rethink your strategy and focus more on the rising stars. They do have more upside, you know. Lorenzo is, what, the ripe old age of *thirty*?" She shudders as if thirty is geriatric in pro ball. Unfortunately, it kind of is.

"Lorenzo is not a has-been. And I will bet you anything anytime, because I can win rising stars too."

She shrugs and gestures to the game. "Can you

though? That's more my thing. Like the new right fielder. He's been on a tear during spring training. Think of the potential—like investing in the next Uber or Lyft." She lifts her nose to the air as if inhaling the scent of money multiplying exponentially.

I do like that particular perfume too. Smells damn good.

I also like a throwdown. "Are you challenging me, Delilah?" I ask, using her last name because it helps me keep her at a distance.

"I am. Since you love to bet." She pauses, purses her lips, then takes her sweet time saying, "Summers."

She says it like she knows all my secrets. She knows enough of them to be dangerous.

"Next big rising star athlete up for grabs," I say. "Let's bet on who wins him."

"Him? You're assuming the next big rising star will be a man." She shakes her head, tsking. "That makes you like all the others."

I blanch at my own faux pas. I ought to know better. I rep plenty of top-tier female athletes. "You know I've never been a chauvinist."

"You haven't?"

I inch closer, getting in her space. "You damn well know I'm not."

She lifts that haughty chin. That sexy, haughty chin I want to slide my thumb across and bite. "Great. Then let's wager. When I sign the next rising star, I get to dictate what you'll wear to the top sporting event in the field."

Fueled by my own excess of confidence, I show my hand now too. "I'll wear a shirt that says *Haven Delilah is the top sports agent in the country.*"

Her brown eyes twinkle like a constellation of stars. "I will take that bet."

I park my hands on my hips. "And if I win?"

"Yes, *if* you win, what do you want me to wear?" The question comes out sultry, smoky, as she juts out a hip and gestures to her lithe, toned frame.

My throat goes dry. My brain goes hazy.

What do I want her to wear?

My favorite outfit on her.

I want her to wear my dress shirt, to button it only halfway. I want her to slink into my room, toying with the remaining buttons, and nibble on the corner of her lip as she gives me a come-hither look.

Whoa. That was out of the blue.

And I've got to recover from that brain malfunction.

I swallow roughly, past the gravel in my throat, jumping off the monkey bars again. "How about you wear my college ball jersey?"

She smiles without showing any teeth then taps my chest. "That's so cute."

"What's cute?"

"How you hold on to your college glory days."

I seethe inside. "Do we have a deal?"

She extends her hand, and we shake. "Of course I will wear your jersey. You were what? A kicker?"

"Try again, sweetheart."

"I wish my memory were better for second stringers."

I shake my head. "Rose Bowl, baby. I won the Rose Bowl. All-American."

She cocks her head to the side. "Rose Bowl is fantastic. But do you really want to go against me in the *who has the bigger trophy* department?"

"Of course not. We all know you have the bigger dick on that count."

Her eyes twinkle. "Why, thank you."

I don't give another inch. Instead, I sidestep. "How's the beer?"

She takes a hearty drink, humming against the bottle, then smacks her lips. "Want a sip? Just to show me what a good sport you are?"

Playing along, I take the bottle, down a gulp, and do my best not to think about her lips. "I'm a great sport."

I hand it back to her, and she takes another drink. "So, congrats on your MVP client. Maybe someday you'll win clients fairly."

It's my turn to roll my eyes. "Are you still bitter? I won Lorenzo fair and square. Sometimes you have to play ball fast."

"Or play dirty ball."

"I don't play dirty ball during the day, and you

know it." I move closer to her, dropping my voice to a husky whisper. "I only play that at night."

A small, traitorous gasp escapes her. Instantly, she snaps her gaze away, her cheeks flushing. *Good.* Hopefully she remembers every sordid detail of our nights together. God knows I can't get them out of my head.

"Then I'll give you the benefit of the doubt about Austin Holloway." She'd repped the hotshot soccer player until he left her a few weeks ago, and I have a meeting with him tomorrow to discuss his representation plans. He's breaking out big-time, and word on the street is he's talking to everyone, including Dick Blaine, aka the guy my boss hates the most.

"I didn't go after him. Didn't have to. Austin called me."

"Don't lie to me, Josh. I swear, if you keep doing this, I will find a new way to make your life hell."

"How are you going to make my life hell? Post nude photos of me?"

"One, I don't have any nude photos of you. And two, how would that make your life hell? You'd probably be happy with it. You're just like every other guy. You all think you look fantastic naked."

"I don't believe you had a problem with how I looked naked."

She steps closer and sets her hand on my chest, leaving a searing imprint. "No, I didn't then. But I don't remember a thing about it now." The national anthem begins, and she turns on her heel to go. But before *"Oh, say can you see,"* I call out quietly to stop her. "The bet, Haven. For the rising star."

"Yes?" She turns toward the flag, putting her hand on her heart.

I do the same. "Who's the athlete?" I say out of the corner of my mouth.

She whispers too. "I guess we'll know when he—"

"Or she," I add.

"—comes on the market."

"So, we'll wait."

"Until we meet again," she says then gives all her attention to the flag.

I do too, shoulders back, though the seashell bra doesn't do much for my dignity. And even though I'm damn glad that Lorenzo won the MVP, this isn't the ideal outfit to be wearing when I run into my ex.

Note to self: next time you see her, wear a suit. Because those drive her wild.

Wait. You're not going to see her again anytime soon.

Also, you don't care if you drive her crazy. Repeat after me—you don't care, you don't care, you don't care.

HAVEN

I like to keep lists of rules for different situations, and after running into Josh at the ballpark, I make a new entry in my personal rulebook.

It's number eight in My Rules for Being a Woman in a Male-Dominated Field.

1. Don't ever be surprised.
2. Remember you will always be thought less capable because you have ovaries.
3. Don't let it get you down.
4. Kick unholy ass every single day.
5. And take no prisoners.
6. You will have to work ten times harder and ten times smarter and be a thousand times more ruthless than your male counterparts.
7. Never let them see you sweat. Ever.

And here is where I add the next rule.

8. Especially that one guy in particular. The one who gets under your skin. The one you wish you'd stop thinking about. Also, how is it possible for him to actually look hot in a luau skirt and seashells? But that's the problem with Josh Summers. The man exudes masculinity even when he's wearing tassels. Riddle me that.

Wait. I need another rule.

9. And of course, never *ever* let on that you can still recall every single detail of the nights you spent with him. Every. Single. Mouthwatering. Detail.

And one more.

10. Do whatever it takes to avoid seeing him at the upcoming Sports Network conference. Surely there's no way he'll be invited to speak as well.

There. That'll do. This list looks perfect.

JOSH

You know how some people have a dessert compartment? Where there's always extra room?

I have a compartment for competition. It never runs out of space.

The next morning as I run in Central Park, peeling off a few miles before I meet a prospective client, I'm going to have to dip into that drawer.

Because *that guy* in front of me? The one decked out in spandex and EarPods? Wearing dark shades and a beanie in the summer, and breaking away from the pack?

Not going to fly.

Don't know him. Don't care. He passed me; therefore, I must pass him.

It's not going to be easy, because he's Hermes, light as air and damn near impossible to catch. He's ten feet in front of me, fifteen, twenty. The dude is aerodynamic and built like he was born for the sport of kicking my ass on the Reservoir path.

I open the competitive compartment, grab some of the reserves, and crank it up.

More RPMs. More speed.

My lungs burn. My thighs ache.

I'm not skinny, not supposed to be. I'm six three, and I played wide receiver in college. That was fifteen years ago, but you can't be slow at that position.

And I wasn't.

So even though the guy trying to show me up— because obviously, it's about me—is built for speed, I'm built for competition. I didn't get to the top of my field without thriving on the fight, the chase, and the wins.

I power along the path, pushing, pushing, till I'm a few feet behind the fellow with the winged feet.

My muscles scream that I'm not that twenty-year-old cocky shithead charging downfield, chasing balls, and making beautiful catches anymore. Plus, there is a helluva lot more ground to cover here than during the average touchdown catch.

And yet . . . here I go, a few more steps.

Then some more.

He's inches in front of me now.

My heart pounds from the exertion, and my reserve tank is nearly empty, but I push past the beanie-wearing, sunglasses-sporting guy I'm about to smoke.

Whoa.

I nearly stop in my tracks, turning to face him. "Austin Holloway?"

He jerks his gaze in my direction then nods in recognition. "That's me. Nice work, Josh, by the way."

I slow to a jog, and he does too, as I break into a smile. "I could tell you I wasn't trying to pass you on purpose, but that'd be a lie." And it's a damn good thing I did. This is competitive compartment serendipity. I point to his newly shaven face. "What the hell did you do with the full beard?"

"I donated it to men who need beards. It's terrible how few can grow a full one, so I wanted to do my part," Austin jokes.

"Good of you to look out for our fellow men."

He drags a hand over his jaw. "Anyway, I heard ladies liked the smooth-faced look these days, so I'm trying this on. Also, I knew you were trying to pass me three minutes ago."

"I had to pass you, man. You passed me. I had no choice."

"Man code. I hear ya. But I do need to tell you something." He drops his voice to a whisper. "I *let* you pass me," he says with a grin.

I shake my head, cracking a smile as my breath comes fast. "In this case, I'm good with that. Because you?" I point at the potential client, the guy I'm meeting in an hour. "You better be faster than I am."

He rolls his eyes. "So much faster. Race you to the coffee shop."

"I guess our meeting is starting earlier than planned," I say.

"Let's do it now."

I take off, going for the element of surprise, but that only lasts so long against the emerging soccer star. This guy is known for his horsepower.

He wins out, outpacing me to Central Park West where he offers me a handshake. "Good job. You're faster than my last agent."

I catch my breath, then ask, "Speaking of your last agent, why didn't it work out with her?"

Austin sighs as we walk up the avenue. "You want the God's honest truth?"

"Yeah, I do. It'll help if we're going to work together."

"I dropped her for a very important reason."

"And that reason is?"

"It's no good having an agent you want to bang."

Wait. Did he really just say that?

"And that's why you left her?" I keep my tone even because this is important and I want to make sure I have it right.

"Yeah, and the reason I called you. No offense, Summers. I'm sure you're a good-looking guy, but I don't want to get you in bed. Or Dick Blaine for that matter." Then he flashes the grin fans seem to love. "But don't worry—so far, I like you better than Blaine."

I rein in a cringe. "Thanks."

This is exactly what Haven predicted she'd encounter as one of the rare female sports agents.

"I have a confession," I'd told her late one night when we were curled up together.

"Ooh, do tell."

"The way you are? So tenacious and fierce? Total fucking turn-on."

She'd grinned in her sexy, sensual way. "Is that so?"

"You're like a snow leopard."

She'd play-growled, then her laughter had faded and her expression had turned more thoughtful as she'd trailed her fingertips down my chest. "I have to be a snow leopard. There will be athletes who drop me because I'm a woman. Because they want to sleep with me. Because they don't want to sleep with me. Because I don't want to sleep with them. It'll come down to sex. I hate that."

I ran my hand along her hip. "It won't come down to sex with you and me."

She smiled, wrapped her body around me, and kissed me hard. "But with you, I like it when it comes down to sex."

"Dirty girl," I said, then promptly forgot about the challenges she faced as a female agent and focused instead on her pleasure.

And when she was with me, she let go. Oh, did she ever let go.

I shake away the memory of our fling. It only lasted a few weeks. No reason she should linger in my head.

Now, as I drink coffee with Austin, that conversation leaves a bad taste in my mouth, because she was right. This guy did what she'd predicted—dropped her for the worst fucking reason—and I don't want to benefit from that kind of douchebaggery.

Yet my boss at the agency has made it clear. He wants a top-notch soccer star for our roster. He wants to grow and grow and grow, and soccer is part of that plan.

We sit down at a juice bar of his choosing, and I segue the conversation to the professional, focusing solely on what Austin wants in an agent, and when we're done, he shakes my hand and says he'll be in touch.

I *should* want to hear from him, should want to sign him, but his comments are rubbing me the wrong way.

Only, I can't let her under my skin.

As I head home, I text my good friend Jason. He's my go-to guy for a ton of things, but especially any thorny issues. He runs an advice empire for guys on how to be the best at both business and being a gentleman.

Josh: Question, asshole.

Jason: Answer coming your way, dickhead.

Josh: What would you tell Person A if he wanted to

work with Person B, but Person B said shit about someone Person A used to sleep with?

Jason: Might Person A be you? Just a guess.

Josh: Gee. Maybe.

Jason: And this person you used to sleep with, shall we call her Person H? For Haven?

Josh: Whatever. Yes. How did you know?

Jason: Because of all the people you used to sleep with, she's the one you can't get out of your brain.

Josh: That's not entirely true.

Jason: That's absolutely true.

Josh: Advice, bro. Give me the advice.

Jason: Here you go, *mate*. I would rate the asshole level of Person B from one to ten and decide if you can handle it. More than five is probably a hard pass. Also, as I tell you every time, you should consider—I dunno, call me crazy—sorting through these issues with Person H.

Josh: Never.

Jason: Or you can keep getting riled up by every mention of her.

Josh: I'm not riled up.

Jason: Nooooo. Not. At. All.

Josh: Exactly. Because I'm going to put her out of my mind right now.

Jason: Good luck with that.

At home, I shower and get dressed for the office. Deciding Austin's asshole level is less than a five, I do my best to put Haven out of my mind when I go to work, then shove her even further out of focus as I spend the day on the phone, first with some general managers, clearing up issues for my clients, then catching up with some of my top performers.

I answer a call from Zane Jarratt, an X Games skateboarding star and one of my first-ever clients. He's a zero on the asshole scale, and I love the guy.

"Dude, you rocked that deal with Monster Energy Bull Rider drinks," he announces when I pick up on the first ring. "Not only did they pay me for the ads, but they gave me free drinks. Free drinks! Can you believe it? That's so cool of you to make sure I got the best bennies."

I laugh. "No one enjoys the perks like you, Zane. Glad you like the money too."

"Yeah, it's enough that I'm thinking I can buy a small island for the wifey. But you did say once that was a bad investment."

"It's a horrible investment. Put it in mutual funds, real estate, or your retirement plan."

"You're right. I've got to remember your badass advice: no islands, no ostriches, and no yachts. Good thing I'm afraid of water, right? Or I'd be buying a yacht next. Wait. Do you want a yacht?" Zane loves to give presents. "Why don't you let me do that for you to say thanks for this awesome deal?"

"I don't need a yacht. I need you to keep being smart with the dough you make. Also, the percent you pay me *is* my thanks, so *thank you*."

"Good point. And on that note, *thank you* for making sure I have these free drinks. I have so much energy now, I need to hit the ramps in my backyard skate park."

"Now that—that was a good investment."

"The best!"

When I hang up, I feel mostly reset. Mostly better.

At the end of the day, Ford raps on my door. "Question. What are the chances you'd want to go to Vegas this weekend for me?"

"Are you going to be busy spanking your wife while the lawn boy watches?"

"How did you know?"

"Lucky guess." I lean back in my leather chair as he

flops in the seat across from me, hoisting one leg over the side. Ford has a way of taking up all the space in the room. The man has a big personality, big mouth, big ideas. "Feel free to drape yourself across my furniture."

"Don't mind if I do." He stretches an arm over the back of the chair now.

"Get a pillow. Make yourself at home."

"Don't kid yourself. I have one hidden under your desk."

"Of course you do."

He clears his throat. "So, Vegas, baby, Vegas." He says it like he's Vince Vaughn—the only way to say it, really—and adds an eyebrow wiggle. "You want to go in my place to the sports marketing conference, don't you?"

I'm staring down a brick wall of a schedule. "No. I don't. I have a ton of calls to make and back-to-back meetings. It's nonstop."

Ford flashes me his best *pretty please* grin. "Suite at the Bellagio. First-class ticket. It's all covered. You could take off Friday morning." He rockets his hand like a supersonic jet. "Barely skip a beat."

"Seriously?" The airplane sound effect makes it hard to tell if he is or not. "My meeting list is ten-feet long."

"That's because your star is so damned bright." He's got his deal-making smile on, and if this were anyone but Ford, I'd be worried what he was up to, giving me the full-court press as he continues. "Don't you rep—hmm, let me think . . . oh yeah! The MVP for the World Series? Didn't that bring more clients to our stables?"

I roll my eyes. "It's prime deal-making season. Especially for football."

"I know, I know. But the panel is going to get some great TV coverage. You want to keep that star climbing."

He has a point about visibility. Athletes often want to sign with agents who are high-profile, who don't just turn up at the stadium but show up as talking heads on the sports shows, commenting on the industry. Some agents have natural visibility, like Haven, everyone's favorite ex-Olympian. Other agents need to work to keep up the profile.

Still, I'm required to give my buddy a hard time, even if I'm now more seriously considering his offer. "What am I? Your backup?"

"My understudy. My second banana," he says.

I grab the basketball from behind my desk and throw it at him.

He catches it easily. "As if I'd miss if I could help it."

"As if I'd expect any less from you. Why do you need me to take your place?"

He pulls himself up straight, parks his hands on his knees, and lowers his voice. "Listen, Viviana and I are trying to . . . you know." He makes a rolling gesture like I should draw my own conclusions.

I stage-whisper. "Make babies?"

"Yes."

"And you don't want to take her with you and make sweet love to her in Vegas?"

He shoots me a steely stare.

I hold up my hands in surrender. "You brought it up."

He concedes my point. "Touché. Anyway, this weekend is *the* weekend, if you know what I mean."

"You mean, she's *ovulating*? It's okay. I took biology before law school. I understand the birds and the bees."

He waves me off. "And I know she'll feel better if we're at home."

I slide into my best Al Green voice. "I hear you. The woman needs home-field advantage."

He gives me the finger, as well he should.

"Don't worry, dickhead. I'll cover for you." How could I turn him down now, even with my stacked to-do list? Gravely I stand to salute him. "As God is my witness, I will do my part in getting your swimmers to her eggs. But if you're successful, I want naming rights."

He gazes at the ceiling. "Why, God, why am I friends with this asshole?"

"Because I'm going to be wingman for all the little Ford Grayson sperm. Since I am a rock-star friend, helping you out. Okay, give me the deets on the gig."

"It's a Sports Network conference on sports marketing. And I was doing a panel on how to negotiate your ass off."

"I bet that was the name of the panel too."

"Indeed. Anyway, Sports Network loves you almost as much as they love me."

I raise a finger. "Question. You did want me to do your baby gravy a favor, or not?"

He bows like he's doffing a top hat. "They love you more, man. They love you like Boston loves Brady. There. Happy?"

"You're the man," I say. Ford stands and heads for the door. But before he leaves, I call him back. "Hey, do you think women get short shrift in this field?"

"Is Christopher Nolan the greatest director ever?"

"Obviously."

"There's your answer. We've talked about it." He eyes me thoughtfully, shuts the door, and sits back down. "What's going on?"

I scrub a hand across my jaw, trying to process what's gnawing at me. "I talked to Austin today about representation."

His eyes light up, and he mimes dropping a fishing rod into the water. He knows the big boss wants the shining soccer star. "Are you going to reel him in like a swordfish?"

I sigh. "Don't know. That's not what's bugging me. He said something about Haven. Well, indirectly."

He sets down his imaginary pole. "Ah, the Haven quandary."

"I know, I know."

"You think far too much about her, brother."

Ford doesn't know how deep it goes. He wasn't

around at CMA then, didn't join us from the West Coast till several months ago. And I don't want to explain it. Haven wouldn't want me to. Only Jason and my sister Amy know. I don't let on to my colleagues that Haven and I had an after-hours thing for a couple weeks before she marched out on red stilettos and gave us all the finger.

I don't blame her for how she left. How could I? Management didn't give her the due she deserved.

"It's stupid, but I still feel protective of her from when we worked together. Even though she hates me. Though not as much as she hates Dick Blaine," I mutter, mentioning our shared Public Enemy Number One. He's no longer with CMA. He left to start his own shop six months ago, and he's in the running for Austin too.

"Everyone hates Dick Blaine. Except his clients. They love him because he's a shark and plays by shark rules."

"As in no rules. He hired Vaughn Channing away from us last year. Man, he was a cool cat. I swear Vaughn used to be one of the good ones." The up-and-coming agent had played tight end for San Francisco for two seasons before an ACL tear ended his career.

"There are plenty of good ones, present company included. And I'm sure Haven was a good one, though I never met her. And listen, I get that you feel like you have to look out for her because that's what you did when you trained her at CMA. Because that's how you are with your sisters."

I furrow my brow. There is nothing brotherly about how I feel for Haven. But I say nothing as Ford keeps talking, philosophizing.

"That's how you said you were with them when they were younger. Hell, you still look out for them. It's the same with Haven. You think of her like a sister."

God, no. I don't think of her like Amy, Quinn, or Tabitha at all.

"But Haven's a grown woman, just like you're a big boy. You don't have to be her protector."

"Austin dropped her because he wanted to sleep with her," I say, and it still tastes like vinegar.

"So?"

"So? How is that a *so*?"

"Because it's his goddamn choice. He's the client. I've been dropped, you've been dropped. You think our clients always open up about why they drop us? Who the hell knows? Men *and* women can be terrific assholes, and guess what? That means clients can be too. We don't rep them because they're Mother Teresa."

"Call me crazy, but I don't want to rep assholes."

"You're going to have a very limited client list, then. As long as he has no prison record, doesn't smack his woman, and doesn't drop his kids on their heads, you should evaluate him on his performance. You can't control the other stuff. It's a blessing when we like our clients, like how you dig Zane and how I feel about Cooper."

"Speaking of, how was his wedding?" I ask. Cooper is the poster-boy good-guy quarterback for the Renegades, and Ford talks about him almost like a little brother. "You and Viv were out there the other month, right?"

"He thanked me for all his success in life. Every single victory," Ford jokes. "It was great. My boy is as happy as all the clams in the sea, and that is my point. We can't go to every client's wedding. That's not what we're here for. We're here to do the best we can for their career." He points to me. "You focus on doing the best *you* can for them."

I nod, absorbing his advice. Austin was just being a guy, and he didn't say anything out of line. "You're right. If the asshole scale isn't too high, I should let it go."

"Everything in business is about the asshole scale."

"I can't let him get to me."

"Exactly. Take him on, go to Vegas, and focus on being the badass you are. Besides, I love your Vegas stories. Didn't you win five large ones playing Texas Hold'em when you were there last year?"

"Oh ye of little faith. Try ten."

He grins. "You lucky son of a bitch. Will you put a grand on red for me?"

"How about I put a grand on you getting your swimmers to the promised land. How's that?"

"I like that bet. I like it a lot." He leaves then pops back in ten seconds later, the expression on his face far too sweet for my liking. My hackles go up. "One more thing," he says with that saccharine grin. "Haven will be speaking at the conference."

I groan. "You want me to suffer."

"Why don't you use this as a chance to talk it out? Get rid of the bad blood you two have?"

"Why don't we have trust falls and corporate bonding games too?"

"That's a thought. Also, thanks again."

"Don't mention it," I say, and he leaves.

Briefly, I consider his idea but squash it just as quickly. Talk it out with Haven? I tried when she left. Or, really, I tried to explain what went down.

She wasn't having any of it, and I don't blame her.

But I did what I had to do at the time.

I risked enough on my end too, so I'm all business now. Win some, lose some, move on.

I fire off an email to Dom Pinkerton, affectionately known as the big boss, with an update about Austin, as well as some deals for other clients that are in the works, including a trade for Alfonso Jordan on the Renegades. I also let him know about my attendance at the Vegas conference in a few days.

A few minutes later, Dom calls me to his office.

I stride down the hall and find the Telly Savalas look-alike on his Bluetooth, pacing the corner suite—his standard MO. He never sits. "That's right. Tell him if he tries this shit again, I will find him and wring his neck. Wrap my hands around it and squeeze. But in a loving way, to remind him to fix this right the hell now."

He smiles then turns to me. The call is over.

I proffer a guess. "Reaming out a general manager?"

"Nah. That was the florist. He got our orchid fertilizer delivery wrong. Asshole."

"Yeah. Some balls on that florist."

"You're telling me. The wife and I need a very specific fertilizer if we're going to keep winning the orchid competitions." He runs a palm across the pool ball of his skull. "So, Vegas. Sports Network. You know what I hear about that conference?"

He reaches for his golf club and takes a swing. The man is in perpetual motion. If you sit in Dom's office, you look lazy. Ergo, I stand. Always.

"What do you hear?" I ask.

He wiggles an eyebrow. "That some of Jackson Pierce's people will be in the city of sin. His best friend and his girlfriend-slash-publicist."

"But not the momager?"

He winks, shaking his head.

Instantly, I know what he means—the hotshot twenty-one-year-old is finally ready to move past having his mother manage his sports career. "I'll find them and talk to them. Helluva match, wasn't it? When he won the Australian Open earlier this year."

"Pins and needles. I was on pins and needles," Dom says, connecting with an imaginary golf ball. Looks like a good shot.

I don't tell him he has a nice swing. You don't suck

up to Dom Pinkerton. Not about golf, orchids, or clients you want to chase.

"I'll work the angles. I presume this means you want to be the agency that represents the superstars *and* the rising stars?"

He grins knowingly. "I want *all* the stars. If he signs with Dick Blaine, I will wring your neck too."

I remain stoic. "There is no way we will lose him to Blaine."

"Good." That one word conveys everything Dom doesn't say—*I trusted Dick Blaine, Dick Blaine crossed me, and Dick Blaine stole clients.*

Dom lifts his club and waggles his hips. "How's your mom? How's Amy? How's Tabitha? How's Quinn?"

He hits a beauty, admiring it as we segue from persona non grata to my mom and my trio of little sisters.

Always ask about someone's family.

Always give a shit too.

Because it's the right thing to do, the right way to be.

That was what Dom told me when he hired me. The man loves money, loves making it hand over fist, but he also gives a shit about your family. That's how I am too. Not because it endears me to anyone—if I didn't care about my clients and their families, I wouldn't fake it. That's not how I'm wired. When I ask, it's because I care to the 1927 Yankees and back.

"Great. Keep me posted on Vegas. All is well with Alfonso's trade?"

"Nearly done with it. The terms are fantastic for him."

"And what's the story with Austin? You're not going to lose him to Dick Blaine King of the Strip Clubs, are you?"

"No, sir." I suspect Austin would enjoy the Dick Blaine strip-club client treatment that I abhor, but I've done my homework. "I have something better than nudie bars. I found a loophole in his contract that'll net him more money."

Dropping his club, Dom thrusts his arms in the air. "God, I love hiring Yale Law School valedictorians."

"What can I say? Contracts are my jam."

He cuffs me on the shoulder. "Let's keep it that way."

"Of course. I'll be following up with him shortly."

"I love loopholes even more than orchids. Almost as much as I love money." He picks up his club again and points it at me. "And you're going to be the one to nab Austin."

I guess it's a good thing Austin doesn't want to bang me, then.

4

HAVEN

It's the middle of the workday, and I'm swimming in a sea of deals, but swimming in deals is where I like to be. Even so, I'm the kind of girl who needs girl time, so when my good friend Sloane pings me with a text, I turn away from my computer, and click on my phone, grateful for the chance to chat.

Sloane: Are we still on for our wine-and-painting class this weekend?

Haven: Stop. I don't want anyone to know I'm taking up painting.

Sloane: Well, is someone monitoring your text messages? Otherwise, how else would anyone know?

Haven: Good point. But we should clearly wear masks and disguise ourselves when we go.

Sloane: I'm glad you're not totally paranoid.

Haven: I just don't want anyone to know I have a soft side.

Sloane: I will keep your soft, squishy center a secret. And I will never let anyone know that you can paint a beautiful hedgehog. While drinking chardonnay.

Haven: It's one of the things I'm most proud of—my ability to do nearly everything while drinking vino. Also, my hedgehog was pretty fantastic, wasn't it?

Sloane: Your hedgehog was the best hedgehog ever painted. But especially painted while drinking. :)

Haven: I don't know what I'll miss more—the wine or the painting, because . . . I have to miss the class. Forgive me! I'm speaking at a conference this weekend in Vegas.

Sloane: Is it for your charity?

Haven: No, but Girl Power is kicking ass! Just landed a huge corporate donation from Heavenly Chocolates for funding athletic programs in the Bronx.

Sloane: Go you!

Haven: The conference is actually a sports marketing thing, and I have big plans.

Sloane: Spill. Celine Dion show? Front-row tickets to Magic Mike? Are those the big plans?

Haven: Who has time for entertainment? I'm trying to score some key meetings when I'm there.

Sloane: Aren't you always trying to score meetings?

Haven: Yes. Yes, I am.

Sloane: Your ambition is boundless.

Haven: Yes. Yes, it is. :)

Sloane: I've no doubt you'll be scoring, then. But be sure to have some fun too. I've always enjoyed Vegas.

Haven: Same here. It's kind of crazy, but I think of Vegas as a good-luck charm. I was in Vegas when I signed my first sponsorship deal.

Sloane: Have I ever mentioned you're thoroughly badass for having been on a Wheaties box? I still have a cereal box with you on it in my pantry, by the way.

Haven: Have I mentioned I love you?

Sloane: Yes, yes, many times over.

Haven: Oh fuck.

Sloane: Um. How did we get to "oh fuck" after "I love you"?

Haven: This email I just received. It's from the reporter who invited me on the panel this weekend. Let me forward you this email of oh fuckery.

Dear Ms. Delilah,

I hope this note finds you well. We are so excited about your attendance at the upcoming sports marketing conference. We've had a few last-minute schedule changes, and I wanted to give you a heads-up that we will be moving you onto the Negotiation Skills panel. We have several other esteemed agents on it, including Josh Summers. Can you attend a prep session in advance? How about Friday evening? We could meet at the Lily Bar and Lounge. (No relation!)

All the best,

Lily Whiting

Sloane: That is some epic oh fuckery.

Haven: I was hoping to avoid Mr. Sexy Pants Summers for the rest of my life.

Sloane: It can still be a long-term goal. But for now, what's the strategy when you see him?

Haven: Easy. I wind him up, needle him like bamboo slivers under the fingernails, because I don't want him to think for a moment that I have a soft spot for him, or that I remember how good he is at giving my favorite thing in the world.

Sloane: Ah, the old pretend-you-despise-him routine.

Haven: I do despise him. I also want to grab his tie and tug him into my hotel room. How is it possible to want to sleep with someone you hate?

Sloane: I believe the phenomenon is called hate sex.

Haven: It's one helluva phenomenon.

5

JOSH

As I work my way through the morning crowds at JFK Airport, I catch up with my youngest sister, Amy, and her work woes. "I hear you. But there are a ton of ways to deal with this issue. Jumping ship isn't always the best option."

She huffs, her frustration with her job escalating by the day. "Do I just . . . stay and keep plodding along? That sounds like the yellow brick road to misery."

"It does. But we need to be smart. *We'll* figure out a plan, devise a strategy. Let's get together when I return and discuss it. How does that sound?"

"That sounds good actually." Amy's been stressed for some time about her publishing gig, but I hear a little relief now. "But can you go sans Bluetooth when I see you? Pretty please with a serving of commercial-free World Series on top?"

"Ames, take that back. The commercials pay for

the broadcast rights, and the broadcast rights pay for my stars."

"And your stars pay for everything. Like my grad school."

"Which you rocked."

"Of course I did. I take after you."

"And for that beautiful compliment, I will ditch the Bluetooth when I see you."

"Miracles can happen!"

I laugh. "I need to take off. I'm almost at the gate."

"Fly safely. I hope you can survive all the pandering they do to you in first class."

"It's tough when they wait on you hand and foot, but someone's got to enjoy the warm hand towels. Might as well be me."

"And the warm nuts. Don't forget the warm nuts. Wait. Real quick. Did you get the invitation I sent you to Josie's baby shower?"

I cringe at the mention of a baby shower. "No. Did you send it by carrier pigeon?"

"Email. Like a normal person."

"I hate email," I say.

"How are you a top sports agent again? Don't you need email for your job?"

"I do work email. Personal email is hell. It's like every sports news site I've ever visited is offering me twenty percent discounts and I can't take wading through the shit in the inbox."

"Which explains why you never replied about the baby shower."

"Actually, that only half explains it. One, I never saw it. Two, I love you, and I love our cousin Josie, but I'm not going to a baby shower. I'll get her a gift, but a man has limits."

She scoffs. "Oh yes. Of course. Stand your ground on baby showers."

I smile as I reach my gate. "And now it's time for warm nuts and pampering. I'll catch you on the flip side."

I end the call and the gate agent scans my boarding pass. As I head down the jetway, I switch over to my podcast app and turn on Jason's *Modern Gentleman* show, his guide on how not to be an asshole.

"Today, let's tackle mansplaining. What is it? Are you doing it? How can you recognize it, and when should you shut your piehole?" I listen through my headphones (because I'm not an asshole) to his familiar British accent, which I'm sure helps his cachet as a manners expert. "We have a question from Brent in Chicago. He writes: 'The other week I went on a date with a woman who's run a few marathons. When she told me about her finish times and how she wanted to improve them in the next one, I suggested she should try some different sneakers, and maybe also add sprints into her regimen. Then she accused me of mansplaining! What did I do wrong?'"

I snort at Brent's cluelessness. I know the answer. I've heard it from Jason before.

"Now, gentlemen, before I answer, you might be wondering if Brent is a fellow marathoner. I made sure to ask him that, and he told me that his favorite sport is working out on a stationary bike. So here we go, Brent." Jason takes a pronounced breath. "You're not a marathoner. She is. You're trying to explain to her a subject in which she is far more knowledgeable, or possibly even an expert. That is the very definition of mansplaining, and ladies detest it. As for what you should do differently, I suggest that you . . . wait for it . . . *listen.*"

Laughing, I hit pause so I can show my mobile ticket to the flight attendant, who has the look of an aspiring actor (though that's hardly long odds in New York).

He gestures to the second row. "You're in 2A, Mr. Summers."

I glance toward my seat then quickly scan the first-class cabin. I do a double take, stomach clenching like I've been sucker punched. Because . . . really?

Fucking really?

Of all the gin joints in all the towns in all the world, she walks into mine.

Over there in 4D, it's like the universe is having a field day with me. Long brown hair scooped up in a messy bun, a silky white blouse, and a pencil skirt that undoubtedly has one of those zippers reaching all the way from bottom to top.

What are the odds she'd be on the same flight as me?

High.

The chances were high.

We're going to the same event, speaking on the same panel, and probably staying at the same hotel.

"Did you need help finding your seat, Mr. Summers?"

I glance back at the flight attendant, who's smiling at me like I'm a confused child at the mall hunting for his mommy.

No surprise—I'm standing in the aisle like a dumbstruck fool, slowing down boarding. And still, even with his waiting gaze, I don't answer him, because I'm drawn to *her*.

Haven laughs into the phone while gazing out the window. I didn't expect a laugh. I expected her to be barking orders at an underling—*Get me the Rangers GM, stat, and if you don't get him, call him every ten minutes till he picks up*—but instead, she's speaking to her mother.

"*Mais oui. C'est vrai, maman.*"

My skin betrays me with a sizzle. Fucking hell. I'm turned on by her talking to her mother? What is wrong with me?

Well, that French accent she slips into from time to time is sex on heels.

Also, those heels are pure sex too.

The attendant clears his throat and gestures more insistently to the gray leather seats next to me. "And this is 2A. See? That's how you find it, because here on Delta, we number the rows from lowest to highest."

That snaps me out of my Haven stupor.

"Thanks," I say dryly. I believe I've just been mansplained to.

And, unlike the marathoning woman, I deserved it.

* * *

She doesn't notice me. Or if she does, she doesn't let on. And I'm certainly not going to hop back two rows and chat with her.

I mean, c'mon. Someone's sitting next to her. Some tracksuit-wearing twenty-something guy with headphones as big as dinner plates, watching his tablet and popping warm salted nuts into his mouth. Not that I looked back and checked.

Okay, once, maybe twice, and her head was bent as she tapped away on her phone.

She's probably working, and I should be working. I position my laptop with the top angled halfway so no one can see the screen—corporate espionage is everywhere, so you can't be too careful—and I dive into work emails as the flight settles in at the cruising altitude.

In 2B, a pink-haired woman with kind eyes stretches her arms high over her head then unleashes a loud yawn.

"Oops," she says, covering her mouth like her yawn surprised her.

I smile. "No worries. These seats are like Ambien."

She glances to the back of the plane, then to me. "I

need to stretch my legs before I nap. You don't think they'll mind if I walk back there, do you?"

"Go for it. Do a couple laps if you want."

She smiles. "Thank you. Confession: I don't know the rules of this cabin. It's my first time flying up here. My sister upgraded me. You look like you fly first-class all the time."

I laugh, sliding a hand down my shirt. "It's the tie, right?"

"The tie, the dress shirt, the oh-so-serious expression on your face."

She must have missed my dumbstruck expression from earlier. "No one will mind if you take a stroll."

"Good to know. But if the snack man comes by with the beverage cart, can you grab me a Coke?"

I don't have the heart to tell her she won't miss the snack man, because the snack man will ask her personally twenty times if she needs anything. "Absolutely. I'll get you your Coke."

"Actually, can you make it two? They probably won't mind, will they?"

"They'll be thrilled to get you two Cokes."

She smiles once more, then wanders past the other side of the curtain, and I return to my laptop. A few minutes later, out of the corner of my eye, I spot red.

A red skirt. Red heels. And a stunning silver zipper from the top of the skirt down to the hem.

Haven walks past me and heads into the restroom. I don't think she noticed me.

That won't last long though.

When she emerges a minute later, she's facing me. It takes her a second to register that it's me. Quickly, she schools her expression, like she's donning a cool and collected mask.

She strolls the few feet to me, setting a hand on the newly vacated chair, adopting a casual pose. "Following me again?"

I go with it, as if she's caught on to me. "Yep. I called Delta, posed as a federal air marshal, and asked for the flight manifestos of every plane leaving for Vegas today. Didn't want to miss a chance to be dressed down by you."

She arches a brow. "Dressed down? Interesting word choice. A little wishful thinking, Summers?"

"It's an expression, Delilah. I could also have said *razzed*, *insulted*, or *trash-talked*. But 'dressed down' seemed to fit you best."

"'Dressed down' it is, then." She casts her gaze toward my computer and the angled screen, then leans in close to whisper, "Joshie, were you being naughty?"

"Excuse me?"

She drops next to me in the seat. "You're such a scofflaw. I can't believe you were watching porn on a plane."

I roll my eyes. "I'm not watching X-rated videos on the plane."

She nudges me with her elbow. "Fine. Tumblr. We all know it's one and the same."

"And yet I'm not."

She gives an *if you say so* shrug. "Okay, but you have the whole Tumblr screen angle thing down pat. You dirty boy."

I hold up my hands in surrender. "Yes, you caught me. I was watching Tumblr. Any chance you could grab me a blanket so I can whack off under it?"

"Why bother with a blanket? Just go au naturel."

"You're right. I'll whip it out and rotate the drive head right now."

A laugh bursts from her throat, but she catches it before it goes on too long. "If you insist." She glances to the couple in the row across from me. The woman wears yellow pants, a white silk blouse, and pearls around her neck. She sits stiffly. The man sports a cravat. A pipe sticks out of his sports coat pocket.

Haven drops her voice to a church whisper. "They won't be offended. They're planning on nabbing their fifth time in the mile-high club on this flight," she says, spinning a story about these random strangers, which is something we used to do.

This is better than fighting, so I go along with it. "Please. They're in the double digits."

She studies them, the anthropologist in her element. "True. It's always the ones you least expect."

I tip my forehead to the flight attendant arranging bottles in the galley. "He'll find them though. Bang on the door. Make a show of calling them out. It's his method-acting practice for his next audition."

"For a police procedural."

"Naturally."

She wags a finger at me. "All the more reason for you to be careful. He'll try to bust you for your tawdry little habit."

I swivel the screen in her direction, flicking it open higher. "It's just email. Nothing tawdry."

"I don't know," she says suggestively. "Some emails can be quite racy."

I arch a brow. "Been sending dirty emails, Haven?" As soon as I say it, a semi-truck of jealousy slams into me. Is Haven involved? I haven't heard anything to that effect, but she's a private woman. She kept *us* private. She wouldn't tell me if she was seeing someone.

Now I'm greener than a stack of hundred-dollar bills. I do my best to deflect my feelings, tossing the barbs back at her. "Maybe you want me to bring *you* a blanket."

"Don't be silly," she murmurs, but her tone . . . it's different. Breathy. Bordering on sensual. I cock my head to the side, curious as a thousand cats. Is she aroused by this talk of self-love? If she is, I'm not surprised. She was shameless in that regard, and I fucking loved it.

And just like that, I'm remembering the time she asked me to come to her room when we were traveling. She'd said the door would be unlocked for me at precisely midnight. "It's a fantasy I have. I want to let it play out."

I'd gone to her hotel room, so damn eager for her midnight fantasy.

When I went in, she lay on the bed, her brown hair fanned out on a white pillow. She'd worn one of those skirts that drove me wild, and on top, she only had on a white lace demi-cup bra. Her skirt had been pushed up to mid-thigh, her legs wide open. Her hand played beneath the waistband of her lacy white undies.

I was swallowed whole by desire.

I'd never witnessed anything sexier in my life.

Until she kicked it up a notch.

"Watch me," she'd whispered, letting her knees fall open wider.

As I crawled onto the bed, I groaned so loud the next county could've heard. "You act like it's possible for me to look away," I said as I set my hands on her ankles, gazing at the hottest sight ever.

Right now, I can't look away either. We're sitting here, face to face in two leather seats, talking all around the topic of pleasure. Even if we're joking, even if we're lobbing insults, I still read sex and fire in her eyes, the same wild desire I feel when I get close to her.

It's dangerous. So damn dangerous.

My throat is arid as a desert, and I want to ask, *Do you remember that night?*

But that's not how this works.

That's not how *we* work.

Not now and not ever.

Even before our fling, we weren't soft and supportive coworkers. Not office buddies or laugh-a-minute friends. We were always prickly because she was such a damn provocateur. She thought she knew better than I did, and I made sure she knew I had *one* job: to teach her the ropes at CMA after she'd joined from another agency.

Except we didn't see eye to eye.

We needled, pushed, pulled.

We were a textbook case of friction.

I remember what Ford said the other day. *Talk.*

I don't know that we're ready to hash out the shit that went down before, during, or after our affair, but I know this: I need to get as far away from sex and zippers and memories as possible. So I grab the steering wheel and take a sharp detour, squealing down a side road that surprises even me.

"How's your mom?" That is the *only* safe topic right now. "Is she doing better?"

A soft smile seems to tug at her lips at the mention of the person she adores, the woman she's credited her success to. "She's great. She got an all clear at her most recent appointment."

"That's awesome. There are no better words in medicine than 'all clear.'"

"I know," she says, her voice catching. "I was so worried about her."

Her mother battled breast cancer two years ago, and Haven helped take care of her, bringing her to appointments and sitting next to her during her chemo.

"Understandable that you'd worry. I'm glad she's better though. Your dad must be too."

"He's very happy," she says, then sighs with relief.

"Have you seen them recently? Sunday dinner in Westchester?"

She smiles. "Just last weekend actually. And I took her shopping. We had a blast."

"I bet you did. Is she back to writing her travel blog?"

"She is." When she talks about her mother, her face lights up with a pure kind of joy. "She just went to Niagara Falls and wrote a piece on—" She stops, narrows her eyes, cocks her head. "Wait. Why are you asking about my mom?"

"Because she's your mother?"

Her expression hardens. "Were you listening to me on the phone?"

And this is what I get for trying to play a safe card. "I was not eavesdropping. I heard you say *'maman,'* so I'm asking. And if it was so goddamn private, why were you having the conversation on the plane?"

"I didn't say it was private. I asked if you were listening. There's a difference," she whispers harshly. "And don't act like it's such a strange thing to ask if you were listening. Not after what went down when I left."

"Haven, I had nothing to do with that shit, and you know it."

"Do I?"

"You ought to. And look, all I heard was you talking to her. I wanted to know how she was doing. It was a legit question borne of a legit concern."

She sighs then shakes her head. "I'm sorry. My fault. Sensitive topic. All of it." Her tone softens again. "But thank you for asking. Better topic than Austin or masturbation."

I laugh at her frankness. "Yes, let's not discuss either of those."

"We could discuss our bet," she suggests. "For the next rising star. Or have you forgotten it?"

"I haven't forgotten."

"Good. I don't want you to wriggle out of it. I can't wait to see you wearing that T-shirt singing my praises."

I narrow my eyes, going mano a mano with her. "You're going to look so good in my number eighty-eight jersey."

"You. Wish."

"I do wish. And my wish will come true. So, do you have someone in mind for our rising star bet?"

Her dark eyes shoot *are you kidding* rays at me. "You think I'm going to let on? Not a chance. It'll be obvious when it's time. But don't think for a second it's Austin."

I scoff. "Of course it's not Austin."

She arches a brow then hums. "So you signed him, then?"

I laugh at her cleverness. "Was that your way of trying to find out?"

"Um. Yeah. Duh."

I lift a brow. "Do you really want to know?"

"I do. I really want to know."

I could go full peacock and tell her I signed the guy yesterday. I could make some dig about how I can do a better job than she can. I could strut my stuff and cock-a-doodle-do and tell her he's the latest in a string of clients I'll win.

All of those are better than the truth—that he's one of those athletes I'm not wild about but will manage to rep. That I can't stomach how he talked about her. That I hate that Austin wants to fuck her. That I hate that anyone wants to have her, and I hate that anyone might.

Instead, I do what we always do.

Needle.

Push.

Pull.

"Maybe I did. Maybe I didn't," I say, playing coy.

"Gee, thanks. I'm sure it's so hard for you to tell me."

But just as I'm about to tell her I'm repping him, the actor-turned-flight attendant ambles over. "What can I get for you two? Oh, I see you switched seats, Ms. Delilah."

"I'm heading back to mine," she tells him sweetly. "But white wine would be great."

"And for you, sir?"

"I'll take a whiskey, and I need a Coke for the lady in 2B."

"Coming right up." The flight attendant spins around, heading for the galley.

Haven arches a brow. "A Coke?"

I pat the armrest of her seat. "She asked me to grab one for her."

"You're so nice to perfect strangers."

"Would you like me to pretend you're a stranger?"

She stares at me intensely. "You don't want me to answer that, do you?"

"No. I don't."

"I didn't think so." She sets a hand on my arm. "But thank you for asking about my mother." She points to her seat. "And now it's wine o'clock."

When she stands, I hear Ford's words again. *Talk it out.*

I make a go of it. "If we were strangers . . ."

She jerks her gaze to me. "If we were strangers, what?" Her tone dares me to say something.

"If we were strangers, I would buy you a drink," I say, attempting to play nice.

She gestures to the galley. "I guess it's a good thing they're free, then, in first-class. That means you wriggled out of that."

So much for talking it out.

Trouble is, there's a part of me that likes it this way, likes the not talking it out.

There's a part of me that likes it too damn much for my own good.

6

HAVEN

I would have liked to take him up on that offer. I would have loved to have a drink with him. To talk more. That's the trouble. That's always the trouble. And that means it's time to add a new set of rules to my handy rule book.

On the ride to the hotel, I start a new list of rules.

Haven's Rules for Resistance

1. Maybe next time, don't make a joke about DIY habits.

2. Or maybe just don't laugh at his comebacks on the topic of giving yourself a hand.

3. And don't be so lured in by his family chatter. He was always like that. It is how he was trained.

4. Safer topics to discuss with Josh Summers: The awesomeness of snow. The benefits of composting. France's contributions to culture.

5. Or to be safe, let's just avoid him, shall we?

That's all well and good but there's that little matter of my schedule and what's coming up next. Drinks with him in an hour. But the reporter moderating the panel will be there, so I won't be alone with him when I go to the Lily Bar and Lounge. That means I won't let a single bit of innuendo fall from my lips.

But when I arrive at the bar, I mutter *Merde* under my breath. She's not here. Where the hell is that woman?

No idea, so clearly it's time for whiskey.

7

JOSH

As I exit the elevator, I finish reading the email from Dom telling me that Lucas Weylan, Jackson Pierce's best friend and the de facto head of the tennis star's *entourage,* is supposed to be here at the Bellagio tonight.

The rest of his note reads: *I talked to Lucas earlier. They love sushi, but I presume you know that.*

I reply as I walk: *I do know that. And I will find him and romance him with the freshest raw fish in the city of sin.*

I'm about to tuck my phone away when I spot a message from Lily, the reporter we're meeting tonight, and I read it as I weave past the baccarat tables with their sharply dressed dealers and equally sharp gamblers.

Hello, Josh and Haven! I'm running five minutes late—

please forgive me. Hold a stool at the Lily Bar for me! (No relation!)

That's hardly late at all. But that also means I might have to see Haven solo again.

It's too much to hope she's running late too. Haven is never late. She's always ten minutes early. Just like me.

I enter the Lily Bar and Lounge, an opulent establishment with panoramic views of the swank casino that's my favorite in all of Sin City. That's not only because the Bellagio and I are tight—I won twenty grand here a few years ago in a blackjack tournament. But also it reminds me of one of the best flicks ever: *Ocean's Eleven.* That's the kind of movie that made me wonder if I should have gone into the entertainment business instead of the sports business. But I love sports too much to do anything else but negotiate top-notch deals for pro athletes.

I loved any sport as a kid. I loved playing football in college.

And I love striking deals for ballplayers as an adult.

Sports has always been my happy zone, and the reason long work hours feel short to me.

I make my way across the bar, girding myself for more torture in the form of Haven. Patrons drape across plush ottomans and velvet lounges, and electronic music pipes through the place, but it's not too loud. It's just right for background music.

Haven is perched on a stool, a glass of scotch in her hand. She's changed from the flight. She's wearing a simple black dress with no visible zipper.

Shame.

Wait. No, that's a good thing. One less distraction.

With a now-familiar cocktail of dread and desire in my stomach, I stride over to her and park an elbow on the bar. "This is my favorite casino."

"Why's that?"

I flash her my best movie-star grin. *"You've got three pairs. You can't have six cards! You can't have six cards in a five-card game."*

She regards me inquisitively, then snaps her fingers. "Brad Pitt. *Ocean's Eleven*."

"One of the top-five best flicks ever."

"And the reason this is your favorite?"

"I'd say that's reason enough."

She raises her glass. "Good reason. Good movie," she says, then downs more of the amber liquid. She sets the glass on the bar and gives me a plastered-on smile. "How was your day?"

I drag a hand through my hair. "We don't need to do this."

"Do what?"

"The bullshit banter. The banter at all."

She breathes an over-the-top sigh of relief. "Oh, thank God. I was so worried we were bound by some rules I wasn't aware of."

Another veiled, or not so veiled, reference to the rules CMA has about promotions and how they're voted on.

I shoot her a look, then I force myself to stare anywhere else but her carved cheekbones, her full lips, her deep brown eyes. I scan the crowd, counting gobs of men and women, men and men, women and women. They're dressed down and dressed up to the nines. They're drinking and laughing and chatting.

None of them look like they want to cut each other to tatters.

And maybe it would be better like that.

Maybe it's time Haven and I hashed it out.

Ford could be onto something.

But before I can assemble those words, Haven goes again, with a note of resignation, "Also, we don't have to sit together while we wait for Lily. It's not necessary. We don't have to pretend we're colleagues or that we like each other." She heaves a sigh like the fight is nearly too much for her as well, then takes another swallow of her drink.

My jaw tightens, and I'm desperate to sling a comeback at her.

But Ford's words echo louder.

Talk it out.

"Haven," I say, sitting on the stool next to her, "what would you say to talking it out?"

She nearly spits out her drink, coughing.

My lips quirk up. I can't help but laugh. "It's not that funny."

"You want to talk it out? You never wanted to talk about anything."

"What? That's not true."

She stares at me like I'm an exhibit at the zoo, a giraffe walking on two front legs. "You didn't even try to talk to me about what happened."

I blink, shaking my head. "You didn't want to talk! I called, and you said, quote, 'You better have a damn good excuse, like you were stuck under a bus during the voting.'"

She straightens her shoulders. "And you weren't stuck under a bus, were you?"

"No, but I bet you wish I had been."

The bartender swings by. "What can I get you?"

A whole bottle. An entire barrel.

"Scotch, please." Then I turn to meet Haven's gaze, trying to tamp down my frustration.

"Look," I say quietly, so we don't make a scene. "Lots of things were a mess back then, and you know it." I point from her to me. "We weren't even supposed to be involved."

She crosses her arms. "I know that. But I wasn't your direct report."

"And yet CMA still has a disclosure policy for office romances with employees, direct reports or not. And we didn't disclose it. We were playing with fire. It was only a matter of time before someone found out we were together."

She lifts a well-groomed eyebrow. "*Together?* Were

we together? Seems more like we were fucking on the road."

I seethe, clenching my teeth, and move closer. I get into her space, whispering hotly, "It was more than fucking."

She raises her defiant chin. "Was it for you?"

"Was it for you?"

She stares at me, a cat never taking its unwavering eye off its prey. "What do you think?"

I think I can't bend or yield. I can't let on how much more it was. "You didn't want anyone to know. You made that clear. I respected that. I didn't tell a soul we had a . . ." I cast about for a word that won't offend her—an affair? A tryst? A fling? "A thing."

Her laugh is humorless. "A thing? We were a thing?"

I key in on what matters. "Was it more than a thing to you?"

She parts her lips, and I swear a word starting with *Y* starts to form on her gorgeous lips. But she clamps them shut then reaches for her clutch, snaps it open, and grabs her lip gloss. She glides it over those lush lips then tucks it away. "It doesn't matter what I thought it was. What matters is when my chance came up for a promotion at CMA, I didn't get it. You didn't vote for me. You didn't care enough." Her voice breaks for a fraction of a second before she collects herself.

"That's not true," I say softly. I hate when women

cry. I hate to see *her* cry. I want to make it all better, even though I'm the last one who can.

"Then what *is* true, Josh? You want to talk it out? Let's do it. Because what's true to me is this." She holds out her fingers, counts off on one. "Fact one: when I started at CMA three years ago, I worked with you—in your department."

"And you questioned everything I did," I say as the bartender delivers my drink, and I knock back some needed fuel.

She wastes no time firing back. "You told me to. You told me you wanted me to learn. My last agency was different. 'Ask anything you want,' you said."

"You didn't just ask. You questioned." I set the glass down. "You thought you knew better because you're an athlete."

"You thought you were right about everything because you're a lawyer."

"I know contracts!"

"I know what it's like to get up at four thirty every morning to train and chase a dream!"

I take a deep breath. *Must zoom in on the end game.* Peace, or something like it. "Fine, so we didn't always see eye to eye."

"Always? More like never."

"Always, never . . ." I try to sound light.

She counts on the second finger. "Fact two: After two years of working together, we were staying late one night at the office. You came into my office and argued about a deal. You were so fucking hot when you were mad, and I couldn't resist, so I told you how sexy you looked, and you pounced."

"*We* pounced," I correct her, my body heating up as I recall that night. "It was a mutual pouncing."

"Fine," she says. She knows what went down that night. I went down on her. She went down on me. And then we fucked it out, bent over the oak desk. "And we pounced a lot."

"For two weeks," I add, my voice a little rough, my mind electric with memories. "And you wanted to keep it quiet."

She holds her hands out wide. "Of course I did. Because of fact three: I'm a woman in a male-dominated field. People would say I was sleeping with you to get a promotion."

I shoot her a sharp stare. "Were you?"

She rolls her eyes. "Let's get one thing straight. I don't sleep my way to the top. Not of anything. Not of medal stands, not of sponsorships, and not of jobs. I used my body for winning competitions, not men. You know what that means?"

"What does that mean?"

My skin sizzles. Her lips are inches away from my mouth as she says, "It means I slept with you for one reason only."

Just the mere mention of sleeping together lights me up. This woman . . . it's like she's pouring gasoline on the ground beneath me. One strike and I'll be a raging fire.

"What's the reason?" I rasp, hard as a rock, hot as hell.

She parts her lips in a gorgeous O, one that rattles loose every damn memory of the way she comes— beautifully, epically.

"I wanted to," she answers defiantly.

Three words, and they're perfectly seductive, thoroughly enticing.

"I wanted to over and over and over," she adds, and I might as well wave a white flag because she's won this round. All she's doing now is throwing more kindling on the fire of me, and I'm burning every-fucking-where.

"So did I," I say, my voice nothing but smoke.

"And let's get to fact four: when I was due for a promotion, you recused yourself from voting on me."

I heave a sigh as she hits me where it hurts. "Haven. I had to."

"Why? Why did you take yourself out of the running? You left me with Dick Blaine, who voted to promote someone less experienced, a mid-level agent. And what's Tom done?"

"Little," I admit. Tom Forrester is fine, but that's all I can say about the guy who *stole* Haven's promotion, thanks to Dick.

And, well, thanks to me.

"Dick is a guy most suited to his name," she says.

I speak from the heart. "I didn't know he was going to fill in for me on the promotion vote." It's only first-time promotions that require a vote at

CMA, and I expected it to go well for her. Then our . . . *thing* wouldn't be an issue again. "I had no idea."

"Why did you recuse yourself, then? What did you tell Dom?"

I draw a deep breath.

Because.

I'd gone into his office and told Dom I couldn't vote on her in good conscience. I didn't tell him I slept with her, but I told him I was falling for her, and that I needed to step back from the vote. I couldn't risk everything I'd built at CMA over ten years. I couldn't risk taking care of my sisters, looking out for my parents, helping my mom and dad pay off their mortgage and buying a home at last in Florida. I couldn't burn it all down for a woman, for anyone. If it got out later that we'd been involved at the time, it would look like favoritism. Worse than favoritism. So I did what I thought was right.

"I told him I couldn't be impartial about you," I spit out. That's not a lie, but I hold back the fact that I'd admitted my *feelings* about her. If she'd had any for me, we wouldn't have ended the way we did. She'd have taken my calls. She'd have listened to me.

Instead, she flipped us all the bird and strutted the fuck out of my life. No way am I telling her now that we were more than a fling, that it was more than fucking.

I gesture to her, all professional and badass. "And look at you now. You started your own agency. You're doing great. You were always best when everything fell on your shoulders."

"Are you saying I'm not a team player?"

I go for diplomacy with a side of honesty. "Well, your sport was individual—not team —snowboarding."

She lets out a tiny laugh. "True."

"Look," I say, trying to soften my voice. "I called you after. Several times. You wouldn't take my calls."

"I was hurt. *You* hurt me. Forget the business part of it. What about the personal part? Don't you get it?"

"I hurt *you*? Because I excused myself from voting on your promotion?"

"Yes." She looks away, swallows. Her voice goes unusually small. "But mostly because you didn't respond to my emails."

I jerk my head to her. "What are you talking about?"

"Nothing."

I tuck a finger under her chin and raise her face. "What are you talking about?" I ask again.

She heaves a sigh that's full of all the hurt in the city. "I emailed you. It's that thing people do to get in touch with other people. You've heard of it?"

I let go of her chin. "I didn't get your emails," I say. I wish I had. At least, I think I would have wanted them.

"I didn't send them to your work email."

"Where did you send them?"

She rolls her eyes. "Your personal email."

Oh crap. Oh hell. "Are you fucking kidding me?"

I grab my phone and search for her name. I find it in ... *spam.*

She's right.

There are three emails from her a few days after she quit.

They are short, but clear.

Can we talk?

Call me!

Whatever.

I laugh at the last one. "Very you."

She shrugs. "Whatever."

"Why didn't you text?"

She stares at me like I'm as stupid as a slug. "You had a company phone. You were a company man."

I set a hand on her shoulder, stripping the frustration from my voice, because I get it. I understand why she was upset. "Listen, I did what made sense at the time. I didn't think voting on your promotion was the right thing to do. I couldn't be impartial. I just couldn't. I wanted you too much."

There. That's all I can give away.

Her lips twitch. "Too much?"

"Yes. Every time I saw you. I wanted you *constantly*. So I stepped back. I had no idea the wreckage it would cause, and I'm sorry."

"Thank you for saying that." She takes a breath, perhaps letting go of her anger. Maybe some of it?

I let go of whatever I'm carrying with me too.

"And now here we are." Her tone is an olive branch.

I seize it. "Do you want to move on?"

She laughs lightly. "To agree to be less vitriolic? Probably a good idea. My coach always said to be zen."

My smile spreads of its own accord. "You were the zen-est on the mountain."

"You remember me on the slopes?"

I tap my temple. "Of course I do. Photographic, baby. Photographic. I watched all your runs in the Olympics. And in the nationals and the world competitions too. You were unflappable, powerful, a vision of winter beauty and speed."

Her smile is uncontainable. It's too broad, too big, too real. Seeing it, knowing I caused it, makes my heart do a little jump.

"Look," she says, her tone soft and friendly enough. "We can try to get along, to not hate each other, especially in public. You win big points for the 'winter beauty and speed' compliment."

"Like a snow leopard." I shake my head, correcting myself. "A snow queen."

She waves a hand. "Stop. You'll make me blush."

"So, do we agree to not be enemies?" I ask, wanting to seal our temporary deal.

"I agree."

"One thing though. The client poaching? It has to stop."

"I don't poach. I win fair and square."

"You took clients when you left," I point out.

She lifts an imaginary violin and plays it. "Oh, so sorry. *Excusez moi* for taking my top talent with me."

I hold up my hands in surrender. I suppose she wins this battle. "To moving on."

She offers a hand to shake. "We will endeavor not to be dicks."

"Dicks? Who's trying not to be dicks?"

The sweet feminine voice belongs to Lily, the blonde sports reporter. She's right behind us, and I turn to meet her.

She waves a hand in front of her face. "I won't be a dick either, I promise. Except I was a big dick for being late, and I'm so sorry." Lily seems more flustered than usual, and she's talking more openly than a buttoned-up reporter usually does. Plus, she's got some sort of pink-and-white shopping bag, a fancy thing that looks like it's from a lingerie shop. "I'm just happy you're still here."

"Of course. It was only five minutes, so don't think twice about it. We were early, so we enjoyed a drink and some good conversation. Right, Josh?" Haven meets my gaze. Her goodwill feels genuine. Legitimate. Maybe we have turned the corner.

I raise my glass. "A great conversation. Incredibly revealing."

"Revealing," Lily says, a little giggly. "Actually, can you excuse me for just one second? I need to freshen up. Traffic was crazy on the way over. So crazy. So very crazy." She spins around and heads for the restroom, stuffing the bag from the shop inside a big purse.

I raise an eyebrow. "Are you thinking what I'm thinking?"

Haven chuckles. "That she's laying the groundwork for later tonight?"

"Pun definitely intended."

Haven leans closer, affecting a male reporter's no-nonsense on-air tone. "*And today, folks, we're here to let you know that Lily Whiting is late because she just enjoyed a little shopping before banging. How about that, Susan?*" She pitches up to the female anchor's voice. "*Well, Bob, I say good for her. Now, for the news.*"

I laugh. It feels good, this truce. This segue into a peace accord with someone I'm going to keep running into, like it or not.

I raise my glass, and we toast.

As I knock back some scotch, I spot the prize I've been ordered to catch, moving across the casino floor like a fish in the ocean. I've cast a rod. Now I need to tug on it, but I can't let on, or Haven will pounce like the big cat she is.

The woman hates lies, though, with a passion. I pick the most harmless one. "I need to put in a call to the boss. Be right back."

"Say hi to Dom for me," she says with a wink.

"Yeah, I'll send your love."

As I leave the bar, I sigh in relief that we're not lacing every word with acid anymore. That we're at least a little lighthearted now about what went down.

I only have a few minutes, though, so I zoom in on my goal. In a heartbeat, I'm at the nearby craps table, where I find Jackson's best friend and roommate. I sneak a glance at Haven. She's on her phone. *Whew.*

"Lucas Weylan?" He's a floppy-haired blond dude with gleaming white teeth. He looks like a California surfer, but he's actually an artist from Vermont and grew up next door to Jackson.

"That's me. Who wants to know?"

I extend a hand. "Josh Summers. CMA. How the hell are you? How's the cartooning business going?"

Lucas flinches, cocks his head, then asks, "How'd you know I'm a cartoonist?"

"A good agent knows what makes both an athlete —and his best friend—tick."

The man smiles, the way that says he's impressed. "Business is awesome. I've been working with Nick Hammer on his TV show."

"That man is genius."

We chat a little more, and he tells me that Jackson is taking pictures somewhere in the hotel with his girlfriend.

But Lucas needs to roll the dice, and I need to get back to business. I clap a hand on his shoulder. "I have some ideas for Jackson. I'd love to chat anytime this weekend. You gentlemen up for drinks tomorrow? Sushi dinner? Night out? Alicia's welcome, of course."

"She has a girls' night tomorrow, so all of the above sounds great." He shakes my hand, and we exchange numbers.

I return to the bar, with Haven none the wiser. She's chatting animatedly with Lily, admiring the reporter's sparkling diamond ring, which catches all the light in the casino.

"Be careful, Josh. This ring might blind you," she says.

I pretend to shield my eyes. "It's stunning."

"I am one lucky girl," Lily says, sighing happily. "Especially since my fiancé says he has a special engagement gift for me too."

"And what's that?"

Lily blushes then waves her hand dismissively. "Apparently it's a secret."

"*Ooh la la*," Haven says, sliding into her French accent. "In France, that can only refer to one thing."

Lily's eyes widen with curiosity. "What's that?"

Haven leans in close to Lily and whispers something I can't hear.

The reporter smiles demurely. "A girl can hope." She flips open her notebook, going into business mode. "So, this is what I wanted to chat about tomorrow . . ."

We spend the next thirty minutes prepping for our panel and all I can think is *We pulled it off.* We buried the motherfucking hatchet.

* * *

When we're done with Lily, she says she has to take off for *a thing*, so we say good night and Haven and I stroll to the elevator bank.

I press the up button. Haven shoots me an inquisitive look. "Good phone call earlier with Dom?"

I furrow my brow for a split second but then recover. "Yes."

"Got lots accomplished?"

"I did," I say with a nod.

"And you sent him my best, I trust?"

I roll my eyes. "Yes, of course. He sends kisses back to you too."

"Great. That's always good, to have a successful call," she says as the elevator arrives and we step inside. I press the button for the twelfth floor. She presses the one for the eleventh.

"It is."

As the doors close, she shoots me a smile that doesn't quite reach her eyes. "And how's Lucas?"

I fix my lips in a straight line, going for a full bluff. "Lucas?"

"Did you think I wouldn't notice you talking to Jackson Pierce's best friend when you said you were on a call?"

Damn. She saw me talking to him. *Deflect, deflect, deflect.* "Wasn't thinking about that at all, to be honest."

She smirks. It was the smirk that could launch a thousand snarks. "Want to know what I was thinking?"

"Sure," I say, bracing myself for a new barb as the elevator whisks us up.

She grins like the devil then pats my chest. "I was thinking the bet is on."

"What are you talking about?" I furrow my brow, like I can throw her off the scent.

She chuckles. "You are so cute when you play dumb."

Fuckkkkkkkk.

I say nothing. What *could* I say to that?

"I'd say the object of the bet is evident, wouldn't you?"

I heave a sigh then strap in, offering her my hand. "Jackson Pierce. You're going to look great, eighty-eight."

We shake on it officially. "Get ready to sing my praises at Wimbledon."

I straighten my shoulders. "So we've found ourselves a new rising star to pursue."

"And you'll need to catch up."

"What do you mean?" My stomach drops.

She tilts her head to gaze up at me. "Why did you think I said yes to this panel? I met with him before I saw you tonight."

When we reach the eleventh floor, she steps out then turns back. "Also, the whole excuse you gave? Calling the office then denying it? You can do better. I knew what you were up to the whole time."

"Good for you, connecting the dots. I would expect nothing less. And if the tables were turned, would you have told me what you were doing? I don't think that for a second."

She stares sharply at me. Her lack of a response is her answer.

"That's what I thought. We're both in business. We're both competing for the same fish."

"And I've got one hell of a fishing rod, Summers."

"I told you, Haven. I already conceded. Your dick is bigger."

She lets go of the door and saunters down the hall, stopping at the first door on the right.

I should be thinking about the competition.

The bet.

The all-consuming need to win Jackson.

Instead, I'm thinking of earlier and Haven's three perfect words.

I wanted to.

8

JOSH

It's a Haven lovefest the next day.

I'm not jealous in the least.

Not when Lily gushes on stage during the Negotiation Skills panel over Haven's performance in the Olympic Games.

"That has to help when you're negotiating," Lily says. "The fact that you know what it's like in the heat of the moment, to have everything on the line."

Haven nods crisply. "I do think it helps, and I would urge anyone considering a career in sports marketing to do some research to truly understand the mind of an athlete."

"That's a great point." Lily turns to me. "Now, Josh, how do you get into the mind of the athlete when you're negotiating for them?"

No way am I playing into this mind-set. Time to take the conversation where I want it to go. "That's honestly not my goal, Lily. I don't try to get into the athlete's head. I'm trying to make the deal work for everyone. For my client, first and foremost. But if the deal doesn't work for the team or the marketer or the brand, then it won't come together. My goal is to make it work for all parties."

"Good point. You always want to try to find common ground," Lily says, seconding me.

"A deal isn't always about finding common ground," Haven pipes in. "The key is to be strategic when negotiating. Be tough. Stare down deals as fearlessly as you would a mountain, then haul ass down the hill like you've got nothing to lose. That's how you conquer it. That's what I bring to table: I know what it's like to set everything else aside, to devote twelve hours a day to your body, to your sport, to the competition. I understand that intimately, from deep inside my soul." She takes a beat, meets my gaze, then says, "In many ways, when it comes to agenting, only an athlete can truly understand what an athlete needs."

Sucker punched. She fucking sucker punched me in public.

And it's not like I can point out that I played college ball, because I'd look like an idiot.

I'd look exactly like the type of jackass who puffs out his chest, and says "hey, gold medalist, look at me."

"Whoa." Lily's eyes widen. "I have to imagine Josh disagrees."

You have no idea.

I clench my fists, imagine I'm in yoga, even though I hate yoga, then do my best to channel Jason's advice.

Be calm. Be cool. Don't ever let someone know they got to you.

Fuck that.

The gloves come off.

I lean back, cross my legs, and smile. "You have that on me, Haven. No argument there. I can't compete with a gold medal. But," I say, raising a finger, "I'd argue that a law degree matters more. A helluva lot more. The business is all about deals, and as agents, our job is to strike the best ones. It's not about who can keep pace on the slopes or at the gym. It's about who delivers the deals. Knowing the law is the only thing that helps with that. Let the current athletes make the goals, hit the homers, win the medals. We'll make the best deals for them so they can focus on the field."

A bell chimes, the cue that the panel is ending. Lily jumps in. "There you go. There are two sides to negotiating. Both bring their own benefits."

Lily ushers us offstage, thanking us. "Guys. Wow. That was great. The way you brought such contrasting viewpoints. It's everything I could want in a session. I can't thank you enough for being so vocal and opinionated."

"It was a pleasure," Haven says with a smile then a whisper for Lily, "And I do hope you enjoyed your engagement present."

Lily blushes. "More than I ever imagined I would."

"You go, girl."

I don't even want to ask. They can play their girl games, and I won't care.

I leave before either one of them can say more, and before I say something I regret.

9
JOSH

At dinner with the rising star, I say nothing I regret. I say only things I mean.

I am on fire. I am the motherfucking man. Because I am not letting Haven win this bet, nor this battle, nor the game.

I am playing at peak performance over drinks and sushi then over a few rounds of poker with Jackson and Lucas.

I push Haven out of my mind. Hell, I shove all thoughts of her out the goddamn door.

I laser in on the potential client, and it works. Plus, Jackson is a zero on the asshole scale, and I like that.

At the end of a game of poker, Jackson raises a glass toward me, flashing a smile that makes him look like a young Taye Diggs. "You sure know how to show a couple of guys a good time."

"Glad you had fun," I say.

"But do you think we're having more fun than

Alicia is having at the Magic Mike Live show?" Lucas says, teasing his friend.

Jackson growls. "If that's where she is, there's no way she's having fun."

Lucas cracks up. "If that's where your woman went for the girl's night out, I can guarantee she's having a blast."

Jackson pats his flat stomach and flexes his arms. "I can go toe-to-toe with those Magic Mike guys."

I clear my throat. "Yeah, I don't think it's the toes the ladies are interested in," I deadpan.

Both men laugh, and Jackson points at me. "Oh that's good. That's very good. And you're damn good with business too, Josh Summers. You're making me rethink everything. Every single thing."

I smile. But I don't let myself get too cocky. Everything could change tomorrow. "That's the goal, man. I'm telling you, I will take care of you. Everything you need."

"I'm all for that, man," Lucas says.

"I know, I know. I just need to talk to Alicia."

It's like when the guy test-driving the Ferrari says he needs to talk to his wife. The mention of the woman can kibosh any deal.

But you can't let it. You need to deal with it head-on. "Definitely. Bring Alicia in. Talk to her. I'm happy to chat with her anytime too." That's the key with any overly involved girlfriend or boyfriend. Make them feel welcome, then actually welcome them.

Jackson shakes my hand. "Awesome. Appreciate

that. We will set something up soon. She's the best, man. I am lucky to have her watching my back."

We say good night, and on the long walk back to my room, I fire off a text to Jason, telling him he'd be proud of me for using his scale for assessing business potential.

His reply is classic, long, and sarcastic.

Jason: Dear Diary, Josh Summers here. You'd be so proud of me. I've learned everything I need to know about life from my good friend Jason. He is so smart. And so handsome. I want to be just like him when I grow up. Also, I swear I didn't think about that someone I used to sleep with at all today. Not when I did the session with her. Not before the session. And not after. I don't think about her at all. I'm just thinking about how awesome my buds are. Love, Josh

Josh: You really are a terrific dickhead.

Jason: I'm the best. The absolute best.

I close the text and vow to keep Haven out of my head as I hit the hay.

* * *

Normally, I sleep like a guilty man—easily, quickly, and deeply.

When lights dim in the movie theater, I snooze. Lower the seat on the plane, and I'm down for the count. So at midnight in this Vegas hotel room, with a downy-as-fuck comforter and a mattress that is practically giving my back a massage, I ought to be comatose till the morning light streams in.

Instead?

I'm as tense as a verb form.

I can't stop replaying the panel.

I can't get her out of my head.

How the hell do people deal with insomnia? Reading this thriller is only winding me up more. A bubble bath? Please. Guys don't take baths unless the tub is full of ice and they just threw more than one hundred pitches.

I glance at the time. I have an early flight and back-to-back meetings in New York to finalize the details of Alfonso's trade. I don't have the luxury of insomnia, so I'm going to have to do what I do with every problem I encounter.

Deal with it head-on.

And that problem is one floor away.

I get up, tug on some jeans, pull on a T-shirt, slide my keycard into my back pocket beside my wallet, and drag a hand through my hair. Grabbing the door handle, I stop, turn around, and take a look in the mirror.

Nice. I look damn good, and that's exactly how I

want to look when I see her. Not because I want to impress her. I just want her to always know what she's missing. I'm thoughtful like that.

I head for the elevator, stab the button, and zoom one floor down. I march along the hall, fueled by determination to get to the bottom of her comment today. Why the hell would she say that onstage in front of an audience?

Only an athlete can truly understand what an athlete needs.

When I reach her door to the right of the elevator, I raise my fist to knock.

Wait.

Could she be in there with a guy?

I flinch at the thought, then an unexpected, red-hot fury lashes through me.

I grit my teeth. I need to get her out of my mind. That's why I'm here. To extricate her from my head.

I rap hard.

A few seconds later, she opens the door, just enough to peer over the chain lock. Her eyebrow climbs. "Funny. I don't remember ordering room service."

"Yeah, I'm here with your French fries and tomato soup. Would you like to let me in so I can serve them to you?"

She tilts her head to the side, *hmm*ing, then answers, "I don't think that's what I ordered though. I specifically requested a contrite chocolate cake with humble strawberries on the side. I think you're going to need to try again with a big fat slice of apology dessert."

I point down the hall. "Great. I'll get two forks. I'll even pour two glasses of cold milk, and we can sit and discuss what went down today. But I'm not apologizing for calling you out on your comment, and you know that."

She laughs. "Of course not. Apologies aren't your style."

With steel in my gaze, I answer her. "Nor are they yours. You could say we're a lot alike in that regard."

"Too alike," she mutters, then clears her throat and unhooks the chain. "You really should have brought a peace offering, Summers. But since I'm enjoying how you showed up at midnight to grovel, I suppose I can let you do it. *Proceed. Grovel.*"

The door inches open another sliver.

"I'm not here to grovel. You know why I'm here."

"I can't read your mind." She takes a beat. "That's probably for the best though. I'm sure it's a dark, dark place up there."

"As is yours," I fire back, then I ease up because more bullets won't help. "Look, I'm here because we have things to discuss. Last night we agreed to talk it out at the bar, and then that all fell to hell today. We need to get this shit sorted because, like it or not, we're going to keep running into each other." I stare at her, stone-faced. "Can you open the door the rest of the way?"

She laughs, that husky, smoky sound that once

drove me insane. Still does. Everything she does drives me wild. She's earned her gold medal in getting under my skin.

"But you didn't actually ask to come in," she says. "You just showed up at midnight and knocked. I thought you wanted to have a door conversation. Was I wrong?"

"Fine. I see how it's going to go." I press my palms together in a plea. "Haven, will you please let me in?"

She gives me a saucy little look and purses her lips. "*Mais oui.* Since you asked so nicely. Do come in." That accent sends a bolt of lust straight down my spine. I bet she knows it too. She knew it was my Achilles' heel when I was with her.

Hell, *she* was my Achilles' heel.

She swings open the door, and I step inside.

"*Merci beaucoup.*"

She lifts her chin and gives me a sexy, sultry look. "Oh, have you been working on your French? It seems you've improved. Admit it, Summers. You're trying to impress me. Tell the truth."

My God, she's never getting the truth. She's never going to know what I said to Dom about how I feel for her. I mean, *felt* for her.

Now, though, the truth is, as I stand there in the foyer of her hotel room, taking in what she's wearing, I want her as much as I did before.

With just as much ferocity.

More, actually.

So much more.

She's wearing yoga pants and a T-shirt, and neither of those hides her toned, trim, muscular body. Even her skirts with the sinful zippers aren't as sexy as this—nothing is sexier on this woman than clothes that accentuate her power. Her strength was a gift she treasured and knew what to do with. She nurtured and developed her gift, and that's one of the greatest things anyone can do with a God-given talent—she used it to its fullest.

I rip my gaze away from her arms and legs and look back to her big brown eyes. "You want honesty? Here it is. What the hell? We agreed last night we would do our best to keep the toxic cloud of hate fumes away from us. So why the fuck would you say that when it comes to agenting, only an athlete knows what an athlete needs?"

"*Only an athlete*," she repeats, slipping into that French accent like it's a scarf she can toss on and off. It sends shivers down my arms. "Why does it bother you? You were an athlete too," she adds, but quickly taps her finger against her lips. "You shouldn't feel bad that you don't have an Olympic medal. Just like I don't feel bad that I don't have a law degree, as *you* so thoughtfully pointed out onstage, over and over and over."

"You know a law degree does come in handy with contracts," I say matter-of-factly.

"And you made that clear. *I'd argue that a law degree matters more*," she says in an eerily accurate imitation of me. She taps my chest lightly. "So, really, I'd say we're even."

"'Even'? Why did you say it in the first place?"

"Because she asked me a question. Because I believe it. And because you and I are competitors. You never let me forget it."

But I don't agree with her assessment. "You don't *want* to forget it. You're a fucking Olympic gold medalist. You love competition."

She sighs, conceding my point. "Fine. I do. But you're just as ruthless."

I smile wickedly. "Thank you. I'll consider that a compliment." I take a deep breath. "But we had a truce. We had an agreement."

"Ah, let's review our agreement, then. It's that we could hate each other in private but not in public?"

"The understanding was that we wouldn't publicly try to undermine each other."

She takes a step closer, stepping into that accent again. "So what are we allowed to do in private, then? I'm just not clear on what the rules are. Because the rules seem to change with you all the time. In private we should cut each other? And in public, we suck up? Maybe we should write these rules down."

I can barely think straight with her this close to me, and I'm starting to regret coming to her room. Because she's in my space, and everything about her is a red-hot distraction. "I'm talking about common courtesy. And part of that—"

"Yes? Part of that is what exactly?"

I stop, trying to shake off the absolutely intoxicating effect of her. "Why the hell are you talking like that around me? Are you trying to turn me on?"

She's inches away, and I breathe in all that delicious honey scent. It swirls around my head, toys with my brain, and tangos with my libido.

She arches a curious brow and gazes at me far too seductively for my own good. "Does it turn you on? I didn't realize it did that for you." Her eyes travel up and down my body. "Or maybe that it still does."

I inhale sharply, trying to clear her from my mind, an absolutely futile effort with her so damn close. She *is* my mind right now. She's the only thing in it, on it, and around it, but I have to get her out. "Haven, I thought we were trying to move on."

"I have moved on. Or maybe that's what bothers you so much. That I've moved on, that I'm not the same woman I was a year ago."

I swallow roughly, my throat drier than a desert right now. "I've moved on too."

Her lips curve in a smirk. "That's good to know. Because I would hate to think you were affected by things I say, how I speak, or the scents I wear. Or wait —are you *still* affected?"

She knows I am. She fucking *knows* it. But I know something too. She's not immune. And since she's been getting in my space, I return the favor, moving closer to her. And there it is—her tell. The soft rush of breath.

I grin. *Wickedly.* Then I take the reins from her. "I

think the question is—are *you* still affected? Because when I look at you, when I see the goosebumps rising over your skin, when I see the flush on your chest, and when you do that . . ." I gesture to her mouth.

Her eyes widen. "Do what?"

I brush my finger against the corner of her lips, barely touching her. "When you nibble ever so slightly on your lips. I know what that means."

She swallows visibly. "What does it mean?"

I lift a hand, reach for her face, and cup her cheek. She gasps.

"*That.* It means both of us are completely unaffected. In fact, I bet we're so unaffected that if I kissed you right now, we'd probably not even care."

She slides next to me, up against me, sealing her fantastic body against mine. "I wouldn't care one bit if you did."

"Let's find out."

She lifts her defiant chin, her pretty pink lips parted. "Go right ahead."

I band my arm around her waist—her tight, trim waist—and haul her in close. I drop my lips to hers, and in an instant, the world disappears.

10

HAVEN

I don't break out my notebook right now.

Obviously.

But I take mental notes, fast and furiously, because I don't want to be in my head. I want to be in my body.

I want him in my body, on my body, all over my body.

So I repeat in my head the Rules for Sleeping with the Enemy…

1. Enjoy it!

(What? Did you think I was going to say something else? You're obviously about to do it. You might as well have the time of your life.)

2. Don't let on how much you want this.

(Or that this is literally your go-to fantasy. Shut

up, it's not. Oh hell, he has his hands in your hair. *Dies.*)

3. Whatever you do, don't say his name.

(It'll help you keep your distance. You need distance from him. You know why. Remember this rule above all. No *Oh, Josh*, no matter what.)

11

JOSH

I devour her mouth. I consume her lips. I kiss her till I can't breathe, and I don't want to breathe anything but her.

We kiss so hard our teeth click. She bites the corner of my lip and kisses me so ferociously it's like she's marking me.

Like I'm marking her. There's no way she'll wake up tomorrow without whisker burn.

Good.

I want her to remember me. I want her to recall every single detail of how I'm going to fuck her tonight. Because *I'm going to fuck her tonight.* I thread my hands in her hair the way she likes, the way that drives her crazy, and I tug on those dark strands roughly. She groans, a wild sound, like desire is strangling her.

That's how I feel.

Tortured by the way I want her. Twisted by this

rampant lust.

Only it's more than lust.

It's so much more, and I try to pour all of that *moreness* into the way I touch her, the way I seal my mouth to hers.

But she's just as charged and not content merely to be kissed. She's rubbing her body against me, broadcasting her intention too.

I drop one hand from her hair, cruising down her back, coasting along the fabric of her shirt, then cupping her ass and squeezing.

Her sounds are electric.

Her noises are white-hot.

I break the kiss and haul her up, lifting her so she wraps her legs around my waist. I meet her dirty gaze and growl, "Just so we're clear, I'm going to have you tonight. I'm going to make you come. You're going to say my name so many goddamn times it drives you crazy."

She stares at me, her jaw set, her eyes fiery. "You can make me come as many times as you want, but I won't say your name."

"We'll see about that."

"I guess we will."

"You seem pretty amped up," I say, yanking her closer to my erection.

Her immediate gasp says that she's as wired as I suspected. But just as quickly, she tries to cover it up with a laissez-faire shrug. "I'm just turned on. That's all. It's not you."

I smirk. "Don't lie. You hate lies."

"Orgasms," she pants. "I like orgasms. Nothing more."

Don't I ever know that. She's not going to bend now, but I have the ace up my sleeve, and I'll play it when I need it. Because I know how to play her body.

With Haven wrapped around me like a koala, I walk her to the bed and drop her gently on the mattress. I crawl over her and cage her in with my arms. Her legs grip me, her feet hooked over my back. I lower my pelvis to her, letting her feel what she does to me. "You're not the only one turned on."

She moans. "I guess you *only* want orgasms too."

"So you do *only* want orgasms," I murmur, having fun with her as I grind and press.

She lifts her hips, seeking more friction. "That's it. That's all."

I grin, pressing my lips to the hollow of her throat. "You're *only* doing this because you're turned on, clearly."

"Yes. Just turned on. Generically turned on, that's all." She refuses to give an inch. It's so alluring, the way she goes toe-to-toe with me, even while her body answers with the truth.

"So it's just a general state of . . ." I pause to lower my mouth to her delicious neck and lick a line up to her ear. A long, lingering sigh falls from her lips, and I finish the sentence. "Arousal."

"Yes," she says, all smoky and sultry. "It's been a while."

I pause, absorbing her comment, because that tidbit is quite interesting. Now I need to know exactly how long. Resuming my pace, I push hard against her, unleashing a wild moan from her. Another push. Another moan.

I swivel my hips, signaling how I plan to fuck her soon. "How long?" I demand.

"Long," she says in a broken whisper, trying so damn hard not to give in.

But her body is begging. She's arching against me, bucking her hips, praying for contact, for friction.

This woman. I know what makes her tick. I know how to drive her insane with pleasure. I have her number and I will dial it over and over and all the fuck over with my tongue and my fingers and my cock.

I lower my mouth to her throat and cover her neck with kisses, easing up on the roughness, sliding into slow, gentle ones along her throat.

Her Achilles' heel. Her dirty little secret. She loves it hard and rough and intense, but pepper in a few soft and sweet kisses, and she melts under me.

Right now, she's a puddle of lust, and I love it.

I smile and nibble her earlobe, another weak spot in her resistance. A feathery kiss behind her ear. My breath in her hair. And friction, so much damn friction.

She's writhing and squirming and losing her mind already.

She murmurs, an enticing string of broken

sentences falling from her lips. *That, oh, God, oh my God*, and *yes, yes, yes.*

I groan. I'm charged so goddamn hot I want to rip off her clothes and my clothes and get inside her right the hell now.

But I table my own want. I intend to focus on her and only her. And my God, Haven is so turned on I could dry fuck her, clothes on, and send her soaring.

But I'm not that cruel.

Or maybe I am.

I bite her earlobe and whisper the truth. "It's been a while for me too."

Her eyes float open. "It has?" Her voice is barren, a vulnerable whisper.

Knowing it'll unlock another level of pleasure for her, knowing it'll take us to the next level in bed, I prime her, asking, "You hate lies, right?"

"You know I do."

Grind, push, press.

"Oh God," she groans, and I push up her shirt, sliding my hands along the soft flesh of her belly then dropping my mouth to her delicious skin, kissing a path along her body to her breasts, making her whimper.

It's the best sound ever.

And it's only going to get better when I tell her more. I draw one rosy nipple into my mouth, suck, then let go. "Then here's the full truth. It's been a whole year. A year and a month and a couple days."

The subtext is crystal clear.

She pushes up on her elbows. "Don't lie to me," she says, all needy and desperate.

I meet her gaze straight on. "It's not a lie. Last time was you."

She grabs my face, stares into my eyes like she can read inside my soul. Hers are dark, blazing with desire. She says nothing for a long moment, then her lips part, and she lets out the most delicious gasp. "Same. Same for me. That's why I need to come right now."

"Then I'll get you there. Since I know that's *all* you want."

"I swear. That's all I want."

"Sexy little liar," I murmur. I tug her shirt off the rest of the way, exposing gorgeous, perfect breasts I could spend all night kissing and sucking.

But I have other plans.

Because Haven Delilah is a pleasure-seeker.

She's an orgasm-chaser.

And she lets go in bed like I've never seen.

I yank off her yoga pants then take a moment to admire her white lace panties. "My favorite," I murmur, dragging my finger against the wet panel. Her knees fall open, an invitation.

"I know," she whispers and closes her eyes like she can't bear for me to see her face when she admits that she wants me.

That she wore these for me.

I tug them off, and my breath rushes out.

She's so fucking sexy and so incredibly turned on.

Pressing my hands on her thighs, I spread her open. She glistens. "Oh, snow queen, you're definitely turned on."

She groans, half in frustration, half in desire. "Just shut up and make me come."

I laugh, blowing a stream of air against the soft skin of her toned inner thigh. She shivers against me and lets out a delicious moan.

"Don't worry," I say. "I know that moan's not for me. It's just because you're horny."

She whispers her answer. "That's it. That's all."

"Of course, snow queen. And all this wetness—it's not for me either."

"Not for you at all."

I press a hot kiss above her knee, and she lifts her hips, asking for more. Asking me to come closer.

"But even so, you should say 'please,'" I whisper, licking a path up her thighs, my lips so close but not quite there.

She practically kicks her feet against the bed, arching against me, her body saying *pretty please with sugar on top*. But her mouth is closed.

I slide my mouth ever so close to her center. My stubble grazes against her wetness. She moans like an animal.

I flick my tongue against her other thigh, working my way closer and closer, teasing and toying.

She whimpers, stubborn as hell. I flick my tongue, taking a taste, just barely, betting her desire will win.

She cries out, and it's fucking perfect. "Please!"

Such a pleasure-seeker.

And I'm a giver.

I oblige.

I kiss her pussy.

And I nearly die of lust.

She tastes better than I remember.

She tastes like honey and desire, and she's so goddamn slippery on my tongue. I could lap her up, drink her down, devour her.

"Yes, God yes," she murmurs, grabbing my hair, clawing at it, like a hungry creature. Her need only ratchets up my own lust. Kicks it up another notch as I lick all that delicious wetness.

She pulls me closer, widens her legs, then thrusts.

Jesus Christ, she's halfway there, fucking my face already.

Just the way she likes it, just the way I like it—wild and hot, nothing held back.

She is abandoned, and I'm the same fucking way with her.

And hell, I'm right there too, turned on beyond words, beyond reason. I lick and kiss, sucking her sweet pussy like it's the only thing I want to do, because God knows it's what I've wanted most for days. Since I saw her at the ballpark, since the plane, since the bar, since the panel.

I give it to her exactly how she likes it.

I eat her like she's dessert, and I crave every last taste. I want every single drop of her pleasure flooding my lips. I flick my tongue against her hard diamond of a clit, fucking and licking and sucking so deliberately that I can barely take the way it makes me feel.

I'm buzzing everywhere. I'm sizzling from head to toe. My dick throbs, desperate for some kind of release. *Soon*, I tell myself, *soon*.

The focus is her right now, and she's going wild. Her hips rock, her hands grab my hair, and her voice rises. "Yes, oh God, I'm close."

I grin, ready to play my ace.

I want her to come. I really fucking do. I want it more than I want tomorrow.

But I also need to remind her of who's doing this to her. Who's turning her world inside out with pleasure.

It pains me to stop, but I do it anyway, right as she's on the cusp. My hands are on her thighs, keeping her legs spread open. "Say my name," I tell her, a clear command. "Say my name and I'll make you come."

She groans. "Fuck . . ."

"You know my name. Say it."

"Damn you."

"Just the name."

Taunting her, I lick a long, lingering line up her pussy, sucking her clit between my lips. Sucking hard. Making her delirious.

The sound she makes hits a new level of desperate on the sex decibel scale.

Then I break away once more. "My name."

"You dick."

"You're getting warmer."

"You big, fucking dick."

"Even warmer. Let me help you along." I give her the pièce de résistance, a full-mouth kiss that makes her cry to the heavens. I stop. "Try once more."

She bucks against me, grabs my head, and moans. "Make me come, Josh. Make me come now."

With a wicked grin, I give her what she wants, devouring her until she flies off the edge, calling my name again.

Oh God, Josh, fuck me, Josh, oh my fucking God.

I'm drunk on her pleasure, intoxicated from her bliss. My mind is a white-hot haze, and all I want is *more*. More Haven, more sex, more *her*.

She slides a hand over her face, through her hair, then back down. Her palm crests over her breasts, her belly. It's the most sensual sight I've ever witnessed— the savoring of her own body as she revels in the aftershocks of release. I can't look away. I want this moment to extend all night long.

And I want something else too.

To bury myself inside her.

To satisfy the ache in me. I *need* her.

When her sounds subside and her eyes flutter open, I shed my clothes, grab her hips and flip her over. "Need to fuck you now."

She needs no direction. She gets on all fours, lowers herself to her elbows, and raises her gorgeous fucking ass.

She surprises me by looking back at me, her

chestnut hair curtaining the side of her face. Even like that, the look in her eyes is stripped bare, patently honest as she says, "I need it too. I need more. Please, give me more."

"With pleasure."

I root around for my jeans and find a condom in my wallet. She watches the whole time, her eyes wide and glossy. Her lips part when I tear open the wrapper, then she sighs so fucking sexily as I roll it on. I wiggle my eyebrows. "You like watching, don't you?"

"You have a nice-looking dick. That's all."

I slide my hand along my shaft. "Thanks. Appreciate the heartfelt compliment. You like my dick, and you think I'm a dick."

"And your dick would look better inside me."

"So impatient." I lean close to her ear and whisper against her neck, "Good things *come* to those who wait."

"I'm not going to wait much longer to come again."

For that sass, I smack her ass, and she yelps then lifts those gorgeous globes higher. So damn impatient.

I get on my knees, rub the head of my cock against her opening, then slide into her. One delicious push is all it takes and I'm filling her. Her heat grips me, and it's spectacular. Pleasure crackles down my spine at the sensation, the utterly intense sensation of her pussy hugging my cock.

I'm buzzed, lit up, lights flashing and whirring everywhere inside me.

I thrust once and nearly lose it. She feels too good.

I still myself for a moment, collecting my racing thoughts so my brain can relay the message to my body to slow the hell down.

I band an arm around her waist, somehow yanking her even closer.

"Oh God, that's good," she murmurs.

"It was always good. It's better than good."

"I know," she gasps, as I start to move inside her. I pull back so only the head fills her, then push in, going as deep as I can. I keep that up for a minute or two, finding a rhythm, savoring the feel. Then I pick up the pace with long, deep strokes that set my body to flames.

They seem to do the same for her, judging from her reaction.

Her back bows, and she grabs the sheets, clutching them, curling her fingers tightly. I cover her back with my body, needing closeness, craving it. Needing to fuck this out.

That's how we'll clear the air. As I fuck her and take her and have her, I bring my mouth near her ear. "This is what you want, isn't it? To fuck it out?"

"Yes," she gasps. "I want it harder. So much harder."

"I know you do. And that's how you're going to get it."

I hold nothing back as I take her the way she wants. Because she wants to be taken. Threading a hand in her hair, I curl the lush strands around my fist and tug.

She cries out, a long, needy *yes*, chased by an *again*.

The lady gets what the lady wants, so I yank hard once more, and I'm rewarded again.

I drive deeper into her, lust and desire slamming into me from every corner. This is our new pace.

Pull, tug, yelp.

Fuck, screw, grind.

We both go crazy, as my hips punch into her, my hand sliding around her waist, my fingers dipping between her legs.

I rub her clit, and she scrabbles at the sheets, her voice rising, her need escalating. "Going to come again," she cries.

"Love it when you come, Haven. Love it so goddamn much," I say as I drive into her.

She's quiet for a second, maybe more. Her body seems to go still, then she calls out, and it's glorious.

My name has never sounded as hot as it does when it's the soundtrack of her orgasm as I'm deep inside her. Her pleasure loosens my own. The world blurs, vanishing into nothing but neon ecstasy as I come inside the woman I thought I hated.

But as I curl my arm tighter around her and bury my face in her hair, I know I was wrong. Inhaling her scent reminds me that I don't despise *this* at all.

Not one bit.

Especially when we both slump onto the bed, spent and exhausted, possibly sated for now. Then she turns to me. She twists around, meets my gaze, and puts a hand on my cheek.

12

JOSH

Her touch is surprisingly gentle.

But even more surprising is how she brings me close, dragging me in for a kiss.

She's tender and sweet, so damn sweet as she kisses me like she's mine, like we do this every night, like this is how we are.

How we *were*.

We were rough and hard, and then we were *this*— lingering, gentle, and more tender than I'd ever have expected.

Her fingers rope through my hair as she sweeps her lips over mine. I'm sinking, sliding into an alternate reality where my fiercest competition, my toughest rival, my *enemy*, is drugging me with delicious, addictive kisses. Each touch is like another shot of endorphins, and each one sends me higher.

I moan into her mouth, my mind unraveling. This

is the kiss that comes after, when we're sated, blissed out, and so damn happy.

She sighs against my mouth, a sensual sound, and for several, intoxicating seconds, I forget everything.

I forget the bet.

I forget the last year.

I forget the shit we've pulled.

The clients of mine she's nabbed. The clients of hers I've grabbed.

The fights, the jabs, the pokes, the prods.

The way it ended.

I forget it all.

Until I remember.

I remember we fight for every deal. We spar for every client. We are locked in the middle of a bet to win the hottest athlete up for grabs.

I need to win Jackson. I have to get him for the firm.

And she wants him for hers.

He doesn't get split in half. He isn't a pie or a slice of cake. One of us will win, and one of us will lose.

And that's why today played out the way it did.

Hell, this woman cut me down in public ten hours ago. I did the same to her.

For all I know, this—tonight, the bed, the sex— could be part of her plan. Seduce me, lure me in. She's a siren, and I'm so easy with her. All she has to do is sing for me, look at me, and I'm in thrall to her.

I yank away, narrowing my gaze. "Is this part of your strategy?"

She blinks, her eyes hazy. "What?"

"To make me forget."

"Forget what? Your name? Are you insane?"

Am I? Maybe I am. That doesn't feel like such a wrong assessment. I feel a little crazy like this. Lying in her bed, tangled up in the sheets, kissing like we are—

I stop the train of thought, shovel a hand through my hair, braking hard.

What the hell is wrong with me? This woman is under my skin, in my head. I can't think straight around her. Can't compile rational thoughts. "No. Nothing. Forget it."

She rolls away, finds her shirt, and tugs it on. In seconds, she's standing, searching for her panties, then pulling them on. She points at me. "You came to my room. Did you forget that, Summers?" I've been relegated to last name only again. "You wanted to *fuck it out*. And we did. So, tell me. What's *my* strategy for you showing up at my door *uninvited*?"

I sit, sighing, scrambling for answers I don't have. "Haven, I didn't mean—"

"Didn't mean what? Didn't mean to suspect me of subterfuge after you stuck your dick in me?"

"Look, I just . . ." I search for words. I search to understand why I'm here, why I'm so drawn to her when I don't even trust her. Or maybe it's that she doesn't trust me. Maybe that's the problem. But whatever it is, I need to find a way to fix it, because I'm pretty damn sure I caused it. "I didn't mean anything."

She parks her hands on her hips and arches one distrustful brow. "Maybe you should *start* meaning what you say, then."

I can't do this again. I can't keep funneling all this frustration, all this energy into my obsession with her. It's messing with my focus, and focus is literally everything when it comes to my job.

My job—the thing that matters.

I have clients, responsibilities, and a boss.

Pulling on my clothes, I try to sort out what the hell happens when I'm near her, this dangerous beauty. When I have my jeans on, I walk over to her, wanting to clasp my hands on her shoulders. But she crosses her arms over her chest.

I get it. I have to fight my way back to *not-hate.* I deserve that.

And maybe the only way over this—the frustration, the anger—is through it.

Maybe this is part of the *talking it out*.

I scrub a hand over my jaw and try again. "I lose my head when I'm with you," I say, admitting the bare truth.

That seems to strike a chord in her. "You do?"

I shrug in admission. "I do. You drive me utterly crazy."

She fires back with "You drive me crazy."

"I guess we're even," I say, a small smirk tugging at my lips.

"Are we? Even? Was tonight about getting even?"

We lock eyes, and I half wish I could find it in me

to sling a zinger. That would be comfortably familiar; that's what we do. But when she looks at me like that, with those deep brown eyes that seem to crave trust and honesty, eyes that tell me she remembers how we were for those few weeks a year ago, nights when we curled up together, when we shared, when we talked —I can't fire arrows. "No. It wasn't about getting even," I say. "It wasn't about anything except needing to get my hands all over you." I clench my fists. "I still want you too much."

She takes a breath, swallows, and closes her eyes. When she opens them, she says in a soft voice, "I want you too, Josh."

There it is. My name. Not a peace offering, but an admission. The confession she only gives me in bed when she's hovering on the edge of bliss. Now I've been given it after, but I don't know what it means. Or if it means anything.

"That's the trouble," she adds, her voice trembling. During moments like this, she's not the ballbuster. She's not the woman who wants to eat me alive. She's simply the woman I want, the woman who wants me too. Except . . . we can't have what we want. "I can't want you like this."

"I know. I can't either," I second her.

"It's dangerous and stupid. It's so stupid."

"It's ridiculously dumb."

She twists her hands in front of her, wringing them. "We can't fall into bed again. We have too much . . . important stuff to deal with."

"Exactly."

She lifts her chin. "So why are we doing this? Did we really just need to fuck it out?"

"Well, you said you were horny," I say, my lips curving up.

That wins a tiny grin from her. "I was," she says, blushing. "I told you it had been a while."

"Yeah, same." But that's all too close to home. I swallow and continue, gesturing to the bed. "This was just about the frustration from the panel. Annoyance. It all bubbled over into sex, right? We're over it. The things that were said. I'm over it. Are you over it?"

She juts up a no-big-deal shoulder. "So over it. Who cares? I mean, look," she says, softening, "your degree helps. You're a good . . . lawyer."

It sounds like it costs her something to say that. Understandably.

"And obviously, you being a world-class athlete can only be an asset." It's true, even if I'm showing my hand, admitting she has something I'll never have. I might pretend my college days equate, but that's not even close. She was the top of her field and has the bling to prove it. I was just one of a few thousand guys good enough to play college ball, but not good enough to go pro. "We both bring something to the table."

There. A truce. The real peace offering.

"Exactly. We're not the same." She gestures to me. "You have your skill set; I have mine. The world is big enough for both of us."

"Definitely. We just needed to clear the air. And we cleared it." I offer a smile that feels nearly legit.

She exhales deeply. "It's all clear."

I wave toward the foyer, where the great midnight fuck-it-out all began when I banged on her door. "Tonight was about getting it out of our systems. That's all."

"That's all it can be. It was pent-up, unfinished business." She laughs. "I mean, a year. *Mon dieu.* That's a helluva long time."

That French again. That accent. But I shake it off. I can't let it unravel me, whisper through me, affect me. "*Mais oui,*" I say. "And now that unfinished business is all finished."

She swipes one hand across the other. "So, we move on."

I nod. Vigorously. "Right. Because it can't happen again."

"It *won't* happen again."

"We're chasing the same clients. We're *always* chasing the same clients. Obviously, we can't be screwing."

"Obviously," she echoes. "And that's all that was. Screwing."

"That was definitely all it was." I make a big show of taking a deep breath, then I fasten on a smile. "Now we move forward and go back to business."

She stretches her arms over her head, like she's exhausted. "And sleep. Nothing like a good O to get me to the land of nod."

I smile, remembering how she slept like a cat after multiple Os. Post sex, the woman would sack out, practically purring. "You love your post-orgasmic sleep," I say.

"I definitely love a solid eight after a couple solid Os." She flashes me a smile too.

Look at us, getting along like a couple of pals. I pat myself on the back for having navigated this new minefield with her and made it to the other side, then glance toward the door. I should go. I *should.*

But I can't quite bring my feet to move.

"And a soak in the tub in the morning," I say. "You loved that too."

"Bubble bath. The whole nine yards."

"I can picture it perfectly." The trouble is, I can picture it *too* perfectly, because I've been there, done that, run the tub for her. I can see her luxuriating in it, slipping a seashell bar of lilac soap over those toned calves, her pink toenails wiggling at me as she pokes them out of the water.

Toes. Fucking toes. I'm remembering her toes fondly.

Get a grip, man.

I need to go.

I need to get out of her zone.

But I remember the asshole levels, and if I leave now, I'm a ten. I can't be the guy who shows up, fucks, and *just* jets.

Something—I need to do something.

I walk to the side of the bed, adjust the covers, fluff

the pillow, and then fold the comforter like I'm from housekeeping. It's not much, but it's better than nothing. I'm no longer a ten. "No chocolate for the pillow, sadly, but voilà."

"And *merci.* Your maid services are much appreciated."

I gesture grandly to the bed. "Sleep well." I pause, take a beat, then add, "Haven."

"I will, Josh." Her soft tone has a hint of sadness that doesn't quite compute.

All the more reason to make myself scarce. I pull on my shirt and head for the door, then stop with my hand on the knob. "Do you still want that contrite cake? I can have some delivered."

Her eyes twinkle. She smiles at me from the foot of the bed then shakes her head. "I appreciate the offer, but I'm more of a cake-for-breakfast gal."

"Another time."

I leave, the door snicking shut behind me. As I return to my room, I'm not sure I've resolved anything.

I'm entirely sure I've complicated matters a whole lot more.

Matters inside my head.

Because when I finally get to sleep, it's not insomnia I'm wrestling with. It's dreams.

Dreams of her.

* * *

The next morning, I'm up before the sun rises, showering off the night before I grab my bag, snag a cup of coffee, and head to the airport to catch an early flight to New York.

Along the way, I call the Bellagio and ask to be connected to room service.

"Good morning from the Bellagio. How can we make your day better?"

"I checked out already but I'd like to place an order of chocolate cake for room 1122."

"Aww, that's sweet to send a cake for breakfast. You're a doll," the woman says.

"That's me."

"Want me to include a note too?"

I cycle through all the things I could say to Haven.

Last night was out of this world.

I'm sorry for doubting you.

Let's do it again. Say, tonight at eight?

But I can't say any of those things. And that last thing *shouldn't* happen.

"Nah, just the cake."

"No worries. Sometimes cake says it all."

"And sometimes cake simply says . . . hope you slept well."

"Would you like to add a glass of cold milk too? It's the perfect pair, and as I always like to say, cake is the best way to make sure I have my daily calcium—with the milk."

"Gotta keep the bones strong."

"That's the spirit."

I finish the order, end the call, and board my flight a little later.

As we're taxiing for takeoff, a note from Lucas pops into my notifications, a reminder that there are bigger things at stake than misplaced lust for someone I once had and definitely, absolutely can't have again.

13

HAVEN

Why did it have to be cake? Especially this decadent, delicious chocolate cake. With a glass of cold milk, this is simply the most indulgent breakfast ever. Cake like this, you can only have after the best sex ever. Like that time I ate it with him that one morning a year ago. When our stomachs rumbled in unison, and he laughed, grabbed the phone, and ordered everything. Eggs, toast, potatoes, cake.

I eat the cake, because it's the perfect meal, then I shower, washing away last night.

When I get out, I don't even stop to check for whisker burn. Except, wait. Is that a new record for whisker burn? I rub a hand over my jaw. And it activates the memories.

His hands sliding through my hair.

His lips crushing mine.

His roughness.

His softness.

His hardness.

The way he toys, the way he teases, and the way he takes.

Stop analyzing every detail and everything he said! That ought to go in your rule book.

Except, I'd like to analyze and dissect and study *that one* comment.

It's been a whole year. A year and a month and a couple days.

What does that mean?

I stare at myself, eyes steely. "It means nothing," I say to my reflection.

Besides, consider the evidence.

He fucks me like he hates me. Well, not entirely. In all honesty, he fucks me like he hates me and wants me and needs me at the same time. Riddle on that.

But I won't spend time riddling on it. I shake it off, and work out hard on the treadmill in the hotel gym, the sweat, and the zone, erasing anything else.

Time to get dressed, go home, and win that rising star like my career depends on it.

There is no silver medal when it comes to winning clients. Besides, silver sucks.

When I land, I find a note from Alicia. A request to meet. *This* is what I need—not that man, not a distraction. A chance to crush it.

I call my mom.

Then, I add one rule to my rulebook: Always call your mom. It's so good to hear her voice.

14

JOSH

The day after I get back from Vegas, Amy waits for me in the new fiction section of An Open Book. With her glasses on and her nose in a hardback, she looks every bit the book editor she is.

Or the disgruntled book editor she is, I should say.

I stride over to my youngest sister, wondering when she'll notice me. Since we were kids, she's always been oblivious to the world when she is lost in a story. The classic bookworm.

But this time, she snaps the book closed with a huff then meets my gaze when I'm a step away. "Ugh."

"What's the 'ugh' for?" I give her the requisite noogie, digging my knuckles into her scalp.

She jumps away. "Ouch. That hurts."

"Thirty-five years of noogies ought to have toughened you up by now."

She peers at me over her red frames, her green eyes incredulous. "Seriously?"

"Seriously, what?"

Standing on tiptoes, she bonks my head. "How were you valedictorian at law school? It's not thirty-five years. You're thirty-five. I'm twenty-eight. It's twenty-eight years."

I laugh. "You're right. Exactly twenty-eight years ago, I started delivering noogies, as soon as you were born." I gesture to the book. "Are you getting that or hating it like the grumpy cat you are?"

She sighs and casts a derisive look at the yellow cover featuring an illustrated couple. "No. I'm not getting it. It's from Owl Landing House Publishers. It's another book I lost out on. Of course it went straight to the top of the charts, a place I could never be. Midlist—I'm the queen of midlist books."

I roll up my shirtsleeves, signaling that it's time for business. "Which brings me to the reason for this meeting. You want me to toughen you up. Let's talk business. Strategize."

"No one better to toughen me up than the most intense, driven, and devoted agent this side of the Mississippi." We head to the café at An Open Book, where she stops at the counter and snaps her sharp-eyed gaze back at me. "Wait. Are you still the most intense, driven, and devoted? I didn't hear a word from you while you were in Vegas. Does that mean you slacked off and played cards all night long?"

Time for my best poker face. I didn't exactly slack off and I didn't hit the tables, but I also wasn't all work.

I tap my chest. "Slap the placard on me. I'm driven and devoted as hell. I worked on Alfonso's trade details on the flight home yesterday. As soon as I returned, I had dinner with Big Kevin C."

"Wrestler?"

"Please. You should watch sports sometime. He's the star forward on the Knicks."

"Don't the Knicks suck?"

I bring my finger to my mouth. "Shh."

She mimes zipping her lips. "I won't tell a soul. I'm assuming no one else in New York is aware."

"Next year, sis. Next year they'll be better. And today I'm meeting with the girlfriend of a new client I'm chasing."

"The girlfriend?"

After we order lattes, I explain how Jackson's girlfriend, as well as his best friend, are intimately involved in all his decisions. Then I bring her up to speed on the potential client, and how Haven's pursuing him too.

"Good luck with that," she says as we sit, drinks in hand.

"Why do you say 'good luck with that'?"

"Tennis is the only sport I follow, because there are some amazing women dominating the game. And Alicia is a girl's girl. She has a pack of girlfriends. She's all about girl power."

That phrase rankles and stirs a new worry. Girl Power is the name of Haven's charity, the one that helps fund athletic programs for underprivileged young girls. If Alicia's a girl-power type of gal, does that give Haven an automatic leg up?

As if reading my mind, Amy asks, "How do you think you'll win Jackson over Haven? Also, didn't you have a thing with her?"

My sister, I swear. She forgets nothing. She's the only other person, besides Jason, who knows what went down a year ago. "Yes, but that's in the past." *Thirty-six hours in the past.* "And, hello, can we talk about you?"

"You started it. I kind of want to know everything now about Jackson and Alicia and this whole bet."

Though I'm curious about gaining further insight from her on the female mind-set of Haven and Alicia's girl-power connection, I shake my head. "We're talking about you. Let's dive into it."

She takes a drink of her latte then tells me her work concerns. I listen, smashing away the occasional thoughts of Haven, of advantages, and of what we did less than two nights ago in Vegas.

We agreed it wouldn't happen again, and it simply can't.

Besides, so what if she has an advantage? All the more reason for me to be ruthless as I focus on what I can bring to the table. That's what I intend to do when I meet with Alicia and Jackson tonight.

After Amy updates me on her work situation, we talk it through and devise a game plan.

"Thank you. That sounds brilliant," she says with a

grateful smile. "By the way, are you going to Josie's baby shower?"

I reach into my back pocket and make a show of opening my wallet. My sister stares curiously. "What are you doing?"

I hold up a just-a-sec finger then continue to root through my credit cards. "Let me see if I can find my man card in here."

She rolls her eyes. "You are so ridiculous."

"No, really. I'll be forced to turn it in if you make me go to a baby shower."

"You act like it's waterboarding."

I find an old credit card and toss it across the table. "It is waterboarding. They do stuff like 'guess what's in the diaper' and 'what position was the baby conceived in.'"

"Someone's been reading up on baby showers," she says, stretching an arm across the table to poke me.

"Of course I read up. I wanted to know what I was turning down. Besides, why do you even want me there? We have two sisters you can drag along. Take Quinn and Tabitha."

"And I'm dragging them along too. But I want you to come." She bats her lashes.

"Why?"

She takes the last sip of her latte, her eyes twinkling with mischief. "Because my friend Peyton is going to be there."

"And?"

"Duh. I want to set you up with her. There. Fine. Are you happy? You got a confession out of me."

I laugh, shaking my head. "You're adorable. But seriously, I can't go. And that's exactly why—you always want to set me up with your friends."

"Well, some women think you're attractive. I mean, not me. Others do. And you're single."

"I am."

She arches a brow then sniffs the air. "Wait. Are you not single? Did you meet a showgirl in Vegas, you devil?" She slugs my arm.

I laugh. "I did not meet a showgirl."

Her eyebrows dance, and she waggles her finger at me. "You met someone. I can see it in your eyes. What happened?"

How is it possible for her to see through me? This is how she got the Haven info out of me in the first place—her laser vision into my head. "Nothing happened."

She studies my face, searching every inch. Then she gasps and covers her mouth. "Oh my God. You saw Haven."

"I did not."

"You did! She was at the conference too. I saw on Twitter. The sports reporter tweeted later about the two of you bringing 'heated points of view' to the stage. What else did you bring a heated point of view to? To her? Did you give her a *heated point of view*?"

Like I said, she's a mind reader. She also kills me,

so I'm cracking up, a giveaway that her *Star Trek* mind-meld worked.

Her smile turns gleefully evil. "Are you back together with her?"

"No. Never. We are never getting back together. We weren't even together in the first place, Ames."

She shrugs impishly. "You say that, yet you did have a whirlwind couple of weeks with her."

She's not wrong. It was an epic whirlwind. And it was also wholly secret, so it was a *surreal* whirlwind. A secret affair, for all intents and purposes.

"And those few weeks proved we're the Yankees and the Red Sox, Batman and Superman, Tweety Bird and Sylvester the cat."

"No." She curls her hands around her mug, her eyes twinkling with mischief. "You're Bennet and Darcy."

I toss a napkin at her. "You want to play lit analogies? We're Valjean and Javert. Holmes and Moriarty."

She stands her ground. "Bennet and Darcy. *Forever.*"

"Bennet and Darcy. *Never.*"

"In that case, you should come to the shower and meet Peyton."

I shake my head. "I can't. I'd probably, I dunno, die. But I picked up gifts for all of us to give Josie."

Her eyes widen. "You didn't!"

I reach for my phone, slide open a photo, and show her the pic I snapped. I took it earlier today in my apartment. With eyes as big as dinner plates, she gawks at the shot of gift after gift from Josie's registry. "Did you buy out her registry?"

"Pretty much. I went online, ordered them, had 'em gift wrapped. I'll even messenger them to her apartment, from the Summers cousins. But I won't go to a baby shower."

She heaves a dramatic sigh, but then says, "Fine." Happily, it seems I'm excused on account of gifts, the fastest way to my sister's heart.

But after I say goodbye to Amy, I breathe a sigh of relief that she didn't ferret out the real reason I don't want to go to the shower.

The reason I don't want to be set up with Peyton.

I'm sure Peyton's a great gal, but the sad, sorry reality is, for the last year, I've had zero interest in any woman other than a certain rival sports agent.

And that's a big fucking problem.

15

JOSH

I have a couple hours free before I head to see Alicia and Jackson, so I decide to burn off some energy with a long walk through Manhattan. As I head up Fifth Avenue, I send a text to Ford.

Josh: Dying here. What's the swimmer report?

Ford: Thanks for your heartfelt concern for my boys.

Josh: Did they arrive at the destination? Did they get scared and run the other way? Are they still on deck?

Ford: You truly have no respect for the sanctity of marriage.

Josh: I have the utmost respect for it. But need I

remind you, your wife admitted she liked spanking at Yankee Stadium, and you then asked me to serve as wingman for your procreation efforts? I believe that entitles me to a report.

Ford: Since you seem to have forgotten the basics of the birds and the bees, let me remind you: WE WON'T KNOW FOR TWO WEEKS. Also, you're an asshole.

Josh: I AM FAMILIAR WITH THE SCIENCE OF THE FEMALE REPRODUCTIVE SYSTEM. But I wanted to rile you up anyway. And I can indeed be an asshole. As proof, let me say this—I don't know how I will get through the next two weeks. Send my love to Viv.

Ford: I'll send your love to the North Pole. Also, thanks, man. Appreciate you filling in for me.

Josh: Anytime.

Ford: Did you and Haven work it out?

As I pass St. Patrick's Cathedral, its spires looming high above me, I reflect on the weekend. All else aside, his advice was spot-on. We did put the past behind us.

Now we are simply two regular old rivals. Nothing more.

Josh: Yeah, we did. Cleared the air. Thanks again. Great advice. And now I'm off to see Alicia and the guy who's going to be the male Serena Williams.

Ford: You never stop working.

Josh: Never ever ever.

And there's no need to stop working when I can devote everything to it once again, thanks to this weekend's *air-clearing.*

When I wander past Central Park and Austin rings, I slide Haven into a drawer in my mind and slide it closed.

"Hey there. How's it going?" I ask.

"This loophole! Damn, you're like the Robert Langdon of contracts. You figured this out. For all I know, my last agent might have too, but hell if I could think past her looks—"

"Just call me a *Da Vinci Code* hero." I cut him off before he can give me another Haven comment. Yes, we all fucking love her.

"Dude, add that to your business card right now,

because you cracked this. This is epic. This is what I wanted. This kind of laser focus."

"I'm glad you're pleased."

"I had some ideas for our next steps," he says. "Can you meet up right now? I'm done with my workout and about to grab a carrot juice."

"Absolutely."

Thirty minutes later, we're talking at the smoothie bar at his gym, and I'm zeroed in on Austin's needs, even as he ogles every woman in spandex and a sports bra, and even when he calls a time-out.

"Be right back. Gotta grab a hottie's number right now."

But I remind myself that, like Ford said, Austin doesn't have to be Mr. Squeaky Clean. We aren't repping nuns and kindergarten teachers. This is my job—to take care of his business needs like the killer sports agent I am.

And that's what I do as we review the plans when he returns.

Yes, this past weekend was everything I needed to reset my mind and get back to work.

* * *

I'm early for my meeting with Alicia and Jackson at The Lucky Spot, but they're earlier.

The bright, bubbly blonde waves me over from their booth in the corner and jumps up when I reach them.

"Look at you! Just look at you. It's so good to meet you," she says, vibrating with boundless energy, like she's hopped up on twenty espressos.

"Pleasure to meet you too."

"I have so many ideas. So. Many. Ideas. It's time, don't you think?" She sits, drops a hand on Jackson's shoulder, and squeezes. "Time to take this man to the next level!"

I'm guessing Alicia was head of the cheerleading squad in high school. Probably college too.

"Let's take him to the stratosphere, where he belongs," I say.

"Yes. *Yes.* You are talking my language." She turns to her man. "Baby, isn't he talking my language?"

Jackson tears his gaze away from the ESPN scroll on the TV. "He is." He drops a kiss to her cheek. "Love you, baby doll. You're the best.'"

"No, you're the best," she says with a big smile. Then she grabs her drink. The ice cubes in it clink forlornly against the glass. "Empty. This is so sad."

"Let me get you another," I offer. "Diet Coke with a slice of lime?"

"How did you know?"

I smile casually. "You don't drink. You've said on Instagram that you like to be one hundred percent present."

Jackson chimes in, draping an arm around her. "My girl is all about the zone. She's always in it."

She smiles with a guilty-as-charged nose wrinkle.

"I do. I don't want any distractions. Thank you for noticing. I totally appreciate that."

At the bar, I grab iced tea for myself and a Diet Coke for her, figuring this woman is going to be on my wavelength. I get the impression that Jackson doesn't care about representation. Only his girlfriend does. She's the one I need to win.

When I return with her drink, she takes a sip then rubs her hands together. "I have a plan. It's going to be fantastic. Jackson's rocket is launching higher, and it's time to move past the momager."

"Alicia," Jackson chides. "Don't be dissing on my mom."

"I'm not dissing her. But, Jackie, it's time. She's been managing you for too long. We need professional representation."

"I know, but be nice to Mom."

She smacks a kiss on his cheek. "I'm always nice to your mom. I took her shopping last weekend on Rodeo Drive, and I Instagrammed it all. And your fans ate it up."

"They did like those pics," he concedes.

"They liked them more than pics of avocado toast."

"And that's pretty much the pinnacle of liking on Instagram," I add.

Alicia clasps her chest. "Yes! An agent after my own publicist heart. He knows Insta, sweetie. This is going to be great. So great. Want to hear my plan?"

"I'd love to."

She takes a deep breath like she's prepping to

deliver *big news*. She grabs Jackson's arm and squeezes. "We're going to the Hamptons for the weekend. Just to chill. Get some sun, play some Frisbee, and work on our tans." She lowers her voice to a whisper. "Take some pics, of course. Because what's more unnerving to the competition than the idea that we're relaxing before his next big tourney, not sweating it at all?"

"That's a brilliant strategy to psyche out his rivals."

She taps her sternum. "I know. My idea."

As if I would think otherwise.

She sits straighter, her smile stretching to the edge of Manhattan. "And we thought . . . wouldn't it be great to have you and Vaughn Channing and Haven join us? Spend a weekend and pitch us on what you can do. Doesn't that sound amazing?"

I'm rarely thrown for a loop. But that's not how business works. Clients don't host battles royal.

I need to redirect this down another, less disastrous path. "Wouldn't you rather—"

"No. I wouldn't rather do it separately. This way, we'll know who's best. It'll be like a reality show without the cameras." Her message is crystal clear—she wears all the pants in the family, and it's her way or the highway. "We saw Haven and Vaughn already, and they're on board. Are you in or out?"

There is only one answer.

I lift the glass of iced tea, take a swallow, and set it down. "I'm all in."

"Great. I'll send a car on Friday for all of you."

I clench my jaw so it doesn't drop off completely. Carefully, I ask, "You want us to take a car together?"

She rolls her eyes. "Of course. I'm not going to make you take a bus."

Jackson squeezes her shoulder. "She's the best. So thoughtful. Love this woman. Just love her to pieces."

"She's the best," I second.

And by "best" I mean the absolute worst.

16

HAVEN

After I get the confirmation from Alicia, I reach out to Sloane. I hate cancelling plans, but I have to chase this deal.

This is the type of opportunity that can vault me to the next level. I grab my phone and write to my friend.

Haven: Forgive me!

Sloane: Bah. Leave me all alone with my wine. And otters. We're painting otters this weekend. Your loss.

Haven: Gah. I love otters.

Sloane: Everyone loves otters. And a good Shiraz. And you're missing both.

Haven: I am the worst friend in the world.

Sloane: I know. I've accepted it. It gives me a chance to beat you in the painting animals race. But enough about the amazing otters I'll paint. Good luck this weekend. And by good luck, I mean good fucking luck resisting Josh "Sexy Pants" Summers.

Haven: It'll be easy this time. Vaughn Channing will be there, and so will Alicia and Jackson.

Sloane: There were people in Vegas too. And yet you didn't resist him.

Haven: That was different. We were in a hotel. It gave off that hotel sex vibe. Anyone would give in.

Sloane: And what if the house in the Hamptons gives off a beach sex vibe?

Haven: See Item 1: Alicia, Jackson, Vaughn. Plus, I devised a whole new plan for Sexy Pants.

Sloane: And that plan is?

Haven: Be friendly. The *grr, I hate you* conversations only fueled the hate sex. So, I need to do the opposite to douse my desire—be kind. :)

Sloane: Kindness is good.

Haven: It is! I'm going to focus on friendship, getting along, and all that jazz. Brilliant, right? Anyway, paint some pretty otters for me this weekend. Send me pics.

Sloane: Tell you what. I'll send you a report on my otters, and you send me a report on your otter.

Haven: Did you just call my lady parts an otter?

Sloane: I did.

Haven: The otter is closed this weekend.

Sloane: As it should be. But just in case someone flips over the 'Closed for Business' sign, I'll be here with my wine and paintbrush, waiting.

Haven: There will be no otter report. And no reports on anything else. Because there will be no sex. No hate sex. And no not-hate sex.

Sloane: So, hate sex with Sexy Pants is a thing of the past?

Haven: Absolutely. The last time made me realize it's so much more than hate sex. And if it happens again, I might tell him everything.

17

JOSH

The car arrives on Friday at eleven thirty.

Alicia said she wasn't sending it till eleven forty-five, but I had a hunch, so when the sleek black vehicle pulls up early, I'm curbside, dressed for the Hamptons.

Fucking Hamptons.

Fucking Alicia.

Fucking jumping through hoops.

And Haven.

But I'm primed today. I'm prepped. It's been a perfect week of *not thinking* of her.

It's been work every day, dinner with Jason and some friends one evening, courtside seats at Madison Square Garden the next, then on another night, a bowling game at a cool retro bowling alley with one of the linebackers I rep. Good friends, good deals, and some entertainment. I even watched *Inception* again while riding the elliptical the other night. Yes, the entire film. That was a helluva work-out. I had a ton of frustration—I mean, energy—to burn.

And not once did I think of Haven.

How could I? My week was packed like a socialite's suitcase for a trip to the south of France.

With my overnight bag slung over my shoulder and aviator shades on, I head for the door of the limo, but the driver scurries around and grabs it first. "Let me get that for you, Mr. Summers."

"Thank you very much," I say then slide into the back seat, expecting to see Haven, since she lives in Chelsea and he'd logically have picked her up first. But she's not here.

Vaughn Channing is though. He's a twenty-some-thing wunderkind who's surprisingly laid back for a guy so driven. I was sure with his combo of chill personality, sharp eye for talent, and dedication to clients that he'd rise to the top at CMA. Instead, he departed for Dick Blaine's agency.

His smile is huge, and he stretches across the limo to shake my hand. "Hey, man, it's been a while. How the hell are you?"

"Good to see you." That's mostly true. The guy did leave to work for someone who's a nine on the asshole scale, and I'm not sure I like that, but I do like Vaughn. "How's it hanging?"

"Low and to the right," he answers.

I laugh. "Better than high and tight."

He grins, and it feels like old times in the office,

when he'd swing by to chat. "Did you see that epic free throw last night?"

We shoot the shit about basketball for a few blocks, since we can always talk sports. *Obviously.* He has the same passion for it that I do, the same love of the game. Vaughn moves on quickly to music, mentioning a nightclub he likes, and he's chattier than I expect, darting between topics almost like he's covering something up.

That possibility nags at me.

I don't need to dig too deep into Vaughn's business, but since I have no problem giving straight talk to general managers, it's time to do the same with a former colleague.

"How the hell is it working with Dick Blaine? Didn't hear much from you after you left. I admit, I was shocked you'd gone to his shop."

He heaves a sigh and drags a hand through his short dark hair. Then he gives a *what can you do* shrug. "Ever make a decision you regret?"

"Gosh. No. Never."

"Yeah, same here."

"So that's not a ringing endorsement of the Dick?"

He blows out a long stream of air. "Look, it's a long story. There was a girl, and yada, yada, yada."

I laugh. "It's always about a girl, isn't it?"

He stretches across the limo to offer a fist for knocking. "It's always about a girl. Girls make you lose your head, don't they? You do things you're not so sure you'd have done otherwise. And then you spend the better part of a year untangling yourself."

"True that," I say, and that's as far as I want to trudge in that minefield. I'm not about to ask for more intel. He's the competition now, and even if we have girl trouble in common, we're both vying for the same prize this weekend.

Wait. I don't have girl trouble. How the hell could I have any girl trouble? I'm single as the day is long, and Haven is not on my mind whatsoever.

Except when we stop at—what the hell?—the W Hotel, I do have girl trouble.

As in, jealousy trouble.

Why are we picking Haven up at a hotel?

Who did she spend the night with? And why isn't he me?

Wait. Hold on. Those thoughts are not allowed in my head. I don't care who she's spent the night with.

She gets in the car wearing casual clothes, no zipper skirt or heels, just a yellow sundress with a pink flower pattern. Her sandals reveal coral-pink toenails.

She's so goddamn beautiful, and I hate the effect she has on me—the way my skin heats up, my throat goes dry, and my heart thunders in my chest.

Her chestnut hair spills out in waves from beneath a straw hat, and everything—every single thing—about the look is in complete contrast to her business attire.

And it's thoroughly enticing in a whole new way.

It's warm and inviting, and so is her smile. She flashes it first to me, saying hi, then she sits next to Vaughn as she sweeps off her hat.

I grit my teeth. *Lucky asshole.*

"Vaughn! How the hell are you?" She throws her arms around him. *Really lucky asshole.* "I haven't seen you in so long."

"A year. Don't I know it. Missed you, girl."

"Missed you too. We need to talk more. Catch up."

Vaughn gives her a *duh* look. "Um. Yeah. I'm missing all your epic advice on girls and gifts and family and every-damn-thing. It's killing me, Smalls."

She pats his arm, and the dragon of envy beats its wings and breathes fire as she says, "Don't you worry, Channing. Your very own advice columnist is here for you."

I clench my fists. Why the fuck is she so chummy with Vaughn? He works for the enemy, the guy who uprooted her chance at a promotion. Was she even close with Vaughn when we all worked at CMA?

A memory surfaces from before those epic two weeks Haven and I were together. A bunch of us went out for drinks, and Vaughn and Haven laughed and joked about the differences between playing professional sports and repping pro ballers.

Is this the whole *only an athlete knows what an athlete wants* dichotomy? The reminder that this is her ace, that she's tight with an agent who's also a former player?

I bet it is.

I bet she's psyching me out.

And I won't let it get to me. I'm done being riled up by her.

As they chat, I grab my phone and answer messages, reminding myself to stay in the zone.

The phone keeps me busy till we're out of Manhattan, and soon Vaughn is yawning, popping in earbuds and saying cars have always made him sleepy. "If I crash, I trust you guys won't draw dicks on my face like my teammates did?"

I wiggle a brow. "Tempting. Very tempting."

Haven holds up her hands. "I make no promises."

He shrugs with a smile. "I'll take my chances." He eyes the entire back seat longingly.

Haven gets the message. "I'll switch."

"Thanks, girl."

As she moves next to me, Vaughn stretches, and a few minutes later, he's out cold.

It's just us.

And I'm just fine.

Doesn't matter why she's chatty with Vaughn. Doesn't matter where she was last night. Doesn't matter if she's psyching me out.

"My mom was in town. And my little brother. I stayed with them at the W," she says, offering up that tidbit as if it's something she wants me to know. And I like knowing it.

"Oh," I say, trying to strip the delight from my voice. "That sounds fun."

"We had a good time. Went to dinner at a new

French place. We found it *almost* as suitable as bistros in the homeland."

"'Almost' is high praise from you," I say, feeling the tug of a small smile as some of the jealousy slinks away.

But there's still the issue of the sleeping dude. I tip my forehead to Vaughn. "So, you're friendly with the competition?"

The corners of her mouth curve up, an amused grin. "Didn't anyone ever tell you to play nice with both friends and rivals, Josh?"

She has me there. "Fair point."

"He's a good guy," she adds, then eyes my khakis and short-sleeve button-down. "Also, I don't think I've ever seen you in Hamptons gear before."

I glance at my getup. "I prefer a suit and tie, but hey, this is better for the weather."

"The casual look works."

It feels like a compliment. A friendly sort of compliment, different than the ones we've given each other in the past.

"Thanks," I say, meeting her gaze. "Your casual look works too."

"Thank you." She leans in closer. "Confession: I love the beach."

"Why is that a confession?"

"Hello? Snow queen here. I can't let my beach love ruin my mountain cred."

I drop to a conspiratorial whisper. "You'll always be a mountain woman to me."

She arches a brow. "You do know how unsexy that sounds?"

I laugh. "Were you trying to be sexy when you brought up your mountain cred?"

"No, actually. But it did sound totally unappealing."

"Don't worry. You still sounded sexy to me," I say. Resistance is futile.

A flush spreads over her cheeks, and she lowers her head. This is the shy side of Haven. It's so strange that she has one. Such a bold woman, but there's a part of her that's still so . . . girly.

And like the rest of her, it's irresistible. I gesture to her dress. "Also, you look . . . really great in a sundress."

She fingers the hem of the skirt. "Thanks." Her voice flutters, as if she likes the compliment. *A lot.* She takes a deep breath, shakes her head like she's shaking something off, then points from me to her. "Also, what the hell is this?"

"What is what?"

"Are we getting along?"

I wink. "No way. We would never get along."

"Right. Never."

"So, that's definitely not what we're doing," I say with a smile.

"That's what I thought. We're just passing the time, right?" she says, a little grin on her face.

"Passing the time on the ride to the Hamptons."

Since *not* fighting with her is going so well, I add, "This whole weekend is odd. Don't you think?"

"It is, and that's why I better win," she says playfully. "Especially since I'm missing my painting class."

I cock my head, intrigued by that nugget of info. "You take a painting class? Are you serious?"

"Surprise, surprise, right? I go with my friend Sloane."

"That's so not you. What do you paint?" I ask, trying to picture Haven in a spattered smock, a paintbrush in her teeth as she studies an easel. The image doesn't quite gel.

"It's definitely not me, but I wanted to expand my horizons. Push myself. Plus, it's wine and painting, so that helps."

I recite one of her mantras. "Wine makes everything better."

"And when I've had a glass or two, I'm convinced my hedgehogs and otters and foxes rock. Want to see them?"

"I would love to." I mean that from the bottom of my heart. This is a whole new side to her.

She takes out her phone, slides a thumb across the screen, and shows me some shots of simple paintings. They aren't Picassos, but they're cute.

"That's impressive. A woman of many talents."

She lifts a brow, a curious look in her eyes. "What's your hidden talent?"

"You know my hidden talent," I say in a dirty tone.

"What do you mean?"

I inch a little closer. "Giving multiple Os."

She trembles. "You are quite good at that." She taps my thigh. "But I meant other talents."

"But that's a good talent."

She meets my gaze, her eyes a little darker. "It's a great talent," she whispers. "But it's not hidden from me. Tell me a talent I don't know about."

I hum, considering, then hit upon it. "Don't tell a soul, but I can do a few kick-ass hairstyles."

"On you?"

"No. Please. On women. Did you forget I have three younger sisters?"

"Why did they teach *you* to do hair when they had each other, plus your parents?"

"I lost a bet in eleventh grade."

She laughs loudly. "You and your losing bets. What was it over?"

"A game of Scrabble. I bet I'd win, but my little bookworm sister, Amy, beat me. She built onto my *E* and spelled 'maximize,' thoroughly decimating me. So, I had to learn to do hair."

Haven flicks a few strands of her lush hair. "So, you could do my hair in a twist?"

The thought sends a wave of heat through me. I nod. "I can do a twist."

Another flick. "A French braid?"

The flames lick higher. "That too."

She nibbles on the corner of her lips. "A ballet bun?"

And I'm roasted. "Yes."

"How about Princess Leia buns?" she asks, defusing the sexual tension.

But only a little, because as I stare at her face, I heat up. "Yes, and you'd look beautiful. Like you do every single time I see you."

And this right here is why I think I'm going to lose the bet, the client, and my whole damn mind.

She holds my gaze, her lips parting, her shoulders rising and falling. "So do you," she whispers.

If Vaughn weren't here . . .

If we weren't rivals . . .

If my phone wasn't buzzing with a text . . .

Fuck.

My phone is buzzing with Dom's text notification sound. I grab it and click on the message.

Dom: Good luck this weekend. Get him for us. Get him.

Yes, the reminder. Business. I need to think of business, not of Haven's hair, or Haven's face, or of the sweet side of her that makes me forget everything else.

I need to focus on the fact that getting along is better than firing arrows. "This is better, right? We'll be able to manage business better without slinging mud at each other."

"It's so much better," she says.

* * *

When we arrive, Alicia greets us with a smile the size of the sky. Decked out in running shorts and a sports bra, she points this way and that, showing us the guest rooms. Vaughn calls dibs on the first one, and Alicia tells him to go for it. She guides Haven and me to the other side of the house.

"That leaves these rooms for you two. Haven, take this one," Alicia instructs.

"Works for me," Haven says.

"And this is for you," Alicia continues, showing me my room.

I'm right next to Haven, a Jack and Jill bathroom connecting the two rooms.

"Just make sure to knock before you go in," Alicia says, then laughs. "Or you'll get more than you bargained for this weekend."

I push out a chuckle.

Haven seems to do the same. "Thanks for the warning."

"Let me show you the view." Alicia returns to the living room overlooking the deck, and we follow her there. She waves to the beach. "I have to run down to the end of the beach and take some pictures of Jackie while the light is perfecto. Be back in two hours." She gestures to the deck. Stairs lead down to the pool below. "You guys can relax or nap or sunbathe.

Or you can enjoy the pool. It's the perfect temp. *Ciao*."

She spins on her sneakers, darts out, and leaves us in the living room, where Vaughn looks up from his phone.

He stretches, then says he has some buds from San Francisco who have a volleyball game going on a mile down the beach, so he's going to join them.

"See you at the pool?" Her eyes are full of questions.

"Yes, the pool," I answer.

I have to go to the fucking pool with Haven. Well, there's only one thing to do to prep myself to handle this.

Inside the guest room, I send a quick text to Jason as I grab my swim trunks from my bag.

Josh: Pray for shrinkage. I'm heading to the pool with Haven.

Jason: One, I never pray for shrinkage. Two, yours is already shrunk.

I laugh then write back.

Josh: That worked. Thank you.

Jason: I'm always here to help.

When I step onto the deck and look down at the pool, the woman I'm trying to resist is stretched out on a lounge chair, wearing a black triangle bikini as she lifts her face to the sun.

I'm officially unshrunk.

18

HAVEN

As I lounge at the pool, I rewrite my rules of resistance. Clearly, they need addendums. Hell, my addendums need addendums.

Since I'm obviously back at square one. The kindness approach didn't work. It only escalated my desire. As well as my interest. And, yes, my feelings.

Herewith, are my new rules.

1. Consider being simply businesslike when I talk to him, rather than flirty.

2. But is that possible? Because that man. That damn man. He can do my hair anytime.

3. Focus on the competition. Get in that competitive zone, and all those other feelings will fade away.

My phone rings. It's the office, and that's perfect – this will

put me in the right frame of mind for when Josh comes down. I'll be businesslike on the phone, and then with him I'll only be businesslike.

19

JOSH

As I walk down the wooden stairs from the deck to the pool area, I hear the tail end of her conversation.

"That sounds great. My fingers are crossed that Wu Media loves the pitch. And be sure to send Sadie a thank you for taking the time to meet with us. Thanks, Jenna."

She ends the call as I reach ground level. The blue tiles on the pool bottom make the water shimmer like sapphires beneath the sun.

"How's Girl Power?" I ask, figuring that should help matters below the belt. It's not like I'm turned on by her charitable organization.

"Great," she says brightly. "My assistant and I were working on some plans to expand our reach and put some new programs in place. There are things I want to do for girls who are totally kick-ass on the field, but I just don't have the money to fund their sports."

"This really drives you, doesn't it?" I park myself

on the lounge chair next to her. Such a brilliant strategy for making my wood less obvious.

"Absolutely. I've seen the power of athletics and teamwork help girls who need a boost. I was lucky my parents funded all my dreams growing up, so this is my chance to give back. It's something I couldn't really do at CMA."

I tilt my head, curious. "Why's that?"

"My time wasn't really my own. I control my own schedule now, so I have more hours to devote to Girl Power. If we hit a few more fundraising goals, then, along with what I can put into it, I can fund the next crop of programs."

"Wow. That's . . . just incredible." I am thoroughly impressed with her dedication. "I knew you wanted to do that, but it's really taken off in the last year. You should be proud."

She straightens her shoulders. "I am. Thank you."

That worked. Boner be gone. But I'm turned on in a different way, one that has nothing to do with sex and everything to do with her heart. Her big, giving heart.

Great. Just great.

Now I'm getting aroused by my fucking admiration for her.

I can't win with this woman. Every little thing she does Svengalis me.

"And on that note, I'm going for a dip." I head to the deep end, and like a man walking off the plank, I jump into the pool, sinking down, down, down, letting my feet touch the bottom, wishing and hoping the water—something, anything—will eradicate the hold she has on me.

When I rise up from the depths, more water sloshes on me than I expect. Ripples. I break the surface, and there she is.

Wet.

Mischief fills her eyes, her hair's slicked back, and her skin is kissed by the water. "Race ya, Summers."

"You're on."

I power my way down the pool, slapping a hand on the shallow side a second before she does. Surely a friendly competition will be the diversion I need.

I kick off, torpedoing to the deep end, unsure of the race's finish line but not caring. I can keep going. This is a perfect distraction. Especially when she catches up and we reach the edge in unison, go under, and push off, freestyling it to the shallow end.

I pull ahead of her—height, longer arms, and that endless reserve of competitiveness help—but as soon as I slap the concrete edge, there's a tug on my foot.

She's right beside me, and I snap my gaze to her. "Interference? Is that how we're doing it now?"

"Yes!" she shouts playfully. I love the delight in her voice.

I smirk then flop over so I'm floating on my back. "All right. You just keep up the illegal play and see how far it gets you."

I kick some water at her. She darts back, grabbing

my ankle again and tugging me under. When I pop up, I flick my hands through the water, splashing her.

She laughs then splashes back as she stands straight up. "You're evil."

"So are you," I say, sinking under, where I nibble on her toes.

She yelps, laughing, and tries to hopscotch away from me. I surface and take a breath, then I sling an arm around her waist so I can toss her over my shoulder and dunk her.

But the second I make contact, I realize I've made a grave mistake.

It's like when you overrun a pass. You can try to correct, but it's damn near impossible.

I overestimated my ability to play nice.

I don't want to play nice.

I want to play dirty.

She's still laughing, but quickly, so damn quickly, her laughter trails off.

Her smile fades as my fingers tap-dance across her skin.

Her hands dart out, and she presses them against my stomach.

Sparks of lust run roughshod over my body. I wrap my arm around her waist more fully.

"Kiss me," I growl.

She closes the inches, sliding her wet skin against mine, lifting her chin, offering those delicious lips to me.

I drop my mouth to hers, and we're not goofing off in the water anymore.

We're not doing anything but the inevitable.

That's how it feels with her. Like this is our true north.

Touching, kissing, tasting—this is our inevitable end point. Anything else is trying to tug a magnet away from its opposite. My body craves her contact. Total contact.

I haul her in closer as she ropes her hands in my hair. Our lips crash together, our bodies collide, and my senses speed into overdrive, firing the same message over and over—*get closer, get closer, get closer.*

Water droplets slide down her cheek and over her lips. I taste chlorine and Haven, and it's spectacular. Nothing can ruin the taste of her. Nothing can change my want for her.

I kiss her deeper, and she climbs me, wrapping her legs around my hips, looping her arms tighter around my neck, pressing and pushing and driving me over the edge.

There is no more shrinkage. There is only growth.

The sun beats down as I consume her lips in someone else's pool, someone else's house.

Somewhere, I'm keenly aware that this is a very bad idea. The thought isn't even in the back of my mind. It's front and center.

Kissing her is a dangerous risk. But it'd take the entire defensive line of the best team in the NFL to stop me now. I'm on a mission, and I want one thing and one thing only.

I break the kiss, panting. "One more time?"

She scans left then right. "Like a final run down the slopes."

We are speed demons, exiting the pool, grabbing towels, and drying off. The empty house echoes, and I send a silent thank you to Alicia for her dedication to golden-hour photos. I'll do one better with Vaughn and send him some craft beer as a thanks for his volleyball buds.

Inside my room, I shut and lock the door. Once it's closed, Haven is on me. Her hands rush down my chest, over my stomach, grabbing at my trunks and pushing them down.

But wet swim shorts aren't the easiest attire to push off. I help her along, practically peeling them down my legs and onto the tile floor.

My cock springs free, announcing its intentions loud and clear.

She wraps a fist around my length and drops to her knees. In seconds, she takes me in deep.

"Fuck," I groan. "Didn't expect that."

She looks up, her eyes blazing. She lets go. "Why not? You know I love your dick."

Hearing that never grows old. I curl my palm around her head. "Then show me how much."

"*Mais oui*," she says. I groan loudly because she's driving me fucking insane. That voice. Her touch. Her mouth.

She's treating me like a king, sucking and kissing my cock, flicking her tongue along the underside. Squeezing with her hand, too, as she blows my mind with her mouth. The sheer pleasure incinerates me. It obliterates all reason, all sense.

It erases the world.

I'm in a prospective client's house, and I don't care that the competition is deep-throating me. I don't care one bit because Haven is on her knees, sucking my cock like it's the source of everything good in the world.

"You're a fucking goddess," I moan as she licks the head then drags my length to the back of her throat. She opens her eyes and wiggles her brows like she's saying, *Yes, yes, I am.*

"A beautiful, dirty goddess," I add as I thrust into her mouth, clasping the back of her head.

I can barely stand how good this feels. How spectacular it is. How helpless I am with her. She moans around my dick, humming, and rocks her hips like she can't help herself. Holy hell. She needs to be fucked. And I need to take care of her, need to bury my cock in her pussy and drive her out of her mind.

Right. Now.

"Stop," I rasp out.

She obeys, looks up, and licks her lips, a goddamn pussycat after a feast. "*Pourquoi?*"

She kills me. She totally kills me.

"You know why."

She shakes her head. "Tell me."

I grab her under the shoulders, haul her up, and look into eyes that look back into my soul. "I need you. All of you. I need to be inside you. I have to have you."

"Then you should have me." She reaches her hands behind her and unties her bikini top. It falls to the floor. Her nipples are still pebbled from the water, and the sight of them sends a shockwave through me.

"Jesus Christ, Haven. Why do you have to be so fucking beautiful?" I ask, dipping my mouth to one rosy nipple and sucking.

"Oh, God. That's good," she whimpers.

I let go and slide my hands to the tiny scrap of fabric between her legs, work it down to the floor, and then admire her nudity. Her curves, her muscles, her golden skin—she's so stunning, my breath catches.

I clasp her hips. "Why? Why the fuck are you so goddamn sexy? Why do you do this to me?"

She grabs my chin, yanks me closer. "You think you're the only one affected? You think this thing between us doesn't make me as crazy as it makes you?"

A rumble works its way up my chest. "How crazy does it make you?"

Her lips are centimeters from mine. No, make that millimeters. I expect her to whisper an answer. Instead, she grasps my hand, guides it between her legs, and shows me.

I burn every-fucking-where. She's soaked.

"*That* crazy," she whispers.

I walk her to the bed, sink down on the edge, and drag her on top of me. "*This* crazy—it's four in the afternoon, and I'm about to fuck you on the job. Need a condom—"

She shakes her head. "I'm still on the pill. And it's only been you."

Those words. *Only been you.*

I'm stepping off a cliff with her. There is no safe landing. I jump anyway, gathering her close, settling her over my thighs. I hold the base of my cock, offering it to her.

She nibbles on the corner of her lips, rises, and rubs her sweet heat against me. I unravel. The sound I make is obscene and necessary.

She slams a hand over my mouth. "Quiet!"

How can I be quiet when she's rubbing the evidence of her need all over my dick? She lowers her pussy onto me, enveloping me, and I'm so fucked when she's all the way on me.

So unbelievably fucked.

I grip her hips, meet her dark gaze, and whisper one word. "*Haven.*"

She shivers, a full-body shudder that runs beautifully from her shoulders, down her arms, to her hips. "*Josh.*"

"Yes," I murmur. "Fucking yes."

Then we're off.

I grab her ass, thrust inside her. All my nerve

endings are alive, invigorated, and my hips move at a wild pace.

Her fingers thread through my hair as she swivels up and down. Up and down. It's frantic and needy, and so fucking powerful.

She drops her head, her face burrowed against my neck, her lips on my skin. She's moaning and kissing my neck, and I can't take it. I can't take the overload of sensations, the prickles of lust, the wild flames of heat. And I can't take her voice in my ear, a sexy little moan, whispering, "I'm about to come."

I sizzle as I bring her down hard, and she cries out, climaxing.

Seconds later, she murmurs a demand. "Give me another."

I'll give her another and another. I'll give her everything.

I slide my hand between her legs, feeling her clit, and stroking until she's whimpering, crying, panting.

She's a hot, needy mess, riding my cock on a pristine white bed in the guest room. I'm sweating with lust, pushed to the brink of white-hot desire as I punch up into her. She moans then unleashes a keening sound, carnal and wild. I've never heard anything sexier in my life. "Baby. You've got to be quiet. You have to be."

Nodding, she lowers her mouth to my neck and bites.

I shudder as her teeth dig in. "Yes, like that, baby," I

tell her. "Just like that. Give it all to me. Give me all your pleasure."

She shakes, and she bites me harder as she comes again. I follow her there, right to the other side, fighting like hell to stay quiet, when all I want to do is throw back my head and roar.

I purse my lips to swallow the sound of losing control.

And I know I don't want to go back.

I don't want to return.

This is where I want to be.

Afterward, when we're flopped down on the bed, I'm the one to haul her in close.

I'm the one to kiss her gently.

I'm the one to pepper tender kisses across her neck, her cheek, her lips.

And she takes each one like it's a gift, receives it like I've given her something precious.

Her hand slides down my back, and it feels reverent. Her touch does so many things to me. It turns me on, it riles me up, and it sends me soaring. And now, it makes my heart thunder like a wild animal in my chest. One that wants to be with her, next to her, beside her.

"More," I whisper. "Give me more of your kisses."

"Take them all," she tells me.

I am ravenous for her. I don't know if I will ever be sated.

Not with her scent in my head, her body curled around me, and her kisses on my lips and in my soul.

We might have come in here for one final hurrah, but as we kiss like we can't ever get enough, this doesn't feel like the last time for either of us. It doesn't seem like the end run down the slopes.

I *should* keep that thought to myself. But when I'm with her, when she's close like this, I can't think rationally. It's too hard to lie or to pretend like she's the enemy.

My rival, yes.

The competition, yes.

But she's also the woman I can't quit.

The woman I don't want to quit.

My lips travel up her neck, leaving a soft trail of kisses in their wake as I whisper, "It doesn't feel like the last time."

"I don't want it to be," she says in a needy rush of breath.

And like that, with her words, I throw in all the towels. I wave all the white flags. I give in to the opposite of hate.

We kiss like we're alone until the end of the world, like nothing else on earth matters.

Right now, nothing else does.

Because I just don't know how to quit her.

Or that I want to.

But when a voice echoes through the house, I have to.

20

HAVEN

Think fast. Alicia is back. Time to MOVE.

Scrambling out of bed, I tell Josh I'm jumping in the shower and he needs to get dressed like he's about to escape the zombie apocalypse. You know, if zombies were fast.

He leaves, and I wash off the smell of sex, get dressed, and swipe on some mascara in minutes.

Deep breath.

There.

No one can tell I experienced the most intense Os of my life. And that's saying something.

Slapping on a smile, I stick to the simplest lie. "Oh hi, Alicia. The water was great, thanks so much for suggesting a dip. It was just what I needed. Now let's get down to business, shall we?"

Well, it *was* what I needed. I *do* seem to need orgasms from him.

Stop lying to yourself. It's more than orgasms you need. It's more than orgasms you want.

The truth is it's so incredibly much more. It's everything. But I can't have everything.

Or really, I can't have anything . . . with him.

21

JOSH

There is a whiteboard in the living room. And colored markers—pink, purple, lavender, and mint green.

Alicia's four favorite shades, because why pick one, she'd said when the games began.

Oh, yes. There are games.

It's Agent Bingo.

Alicia bounces on her sneakers and points at the three of us on the living room couch. "A watchmaker calls and asks for Jackson to be the spokesperson for a new line of rugged underwater watches. You say?"

Is this for real?

"Why the hell would a tennis star promote underwater watches? There is zero connection," I state, going first.

Vaughn chuckles, shouting to the athlete who's in the open-space kitchen whipping up a smoothie with Lucas. "Jackson, are you moonlighting as Michael Phelps?"

"I'm Flipper now," the man of the weekend calls out.

"Or maybe he's going to start playing tennis on a yacht? In which case, I'd suggest modeling life jackets," Haven offers, a clever, unusual answer.

Alicia slaps her knee. "You guys! You guys are too much. I love you all." She clears her throat, straightens, and taps the pink marker against the whiteboard. "But let's dive into this further. Adidas calls. So does Nike. Puma too. How do we evaluate which is best?"

Like you're doing now, I want to say.

"And I ask because . . ." Alicia stops, centers herself, looks to the sky. "Because we want to maximize Jackson's opportunity *now*." She says it with so much vigor, this woman could be a preacher—the fire and brimstone kind.

"That's the name of the game in tennis," I offer. "You have to analyze a deal down to every zero, to every clause. Your biggest revenue growth in this sport comes from endorsements. You don't have the luxury of negotiating a yearly salary like in the NFL or NBA."

"Exactly. The key is to capitalize on media appearances and sponsorship opportunities," Haven seconds. "So ruthless analysis is critical."

"And don't forget digital rights," Vaughn adds. "We gotta secure those for our boy."

And so the three-way battle royal continues.

After the rapid-fire questions, Alicia peels us away

one by one, sitting us on the deck to answer more questions.

She stares at me intensely. "Let's say there comes a time when Jackson's skills are fading. What do you say to him, Josh?"

She seems to think it's a tough question but it's not. I've known the answer since I started in this job post law school. It's why my clients stay with me. "You have to be honest with clients. There is never any point blowing smoke up his tennis shorts. With honesty comes trust, and trust is what matters most."

She rattles off more questions for me, and so it goes the rest of the evening in this strange *Jeopardy!* meets *Family Feud* showdown. We're all in the fishbowl, and it's odd, but it also makes perfect sense.

Our clients are on display every second as they play their games. They have to navigate spectators and media and coaches who pick and pull them apart.

For a few hours, Alicia does the same to us.

I can't say it's my favorite way to vie for work, but I understand the woman's strategy. I respect her sharp eye, her keen mind, and the intensity that's borne from a lioness desire to protect her man.

He seems to need it, because he's a total softy, content to rib and have fun with his friends.

Yes, he needs this woman, and judging from the way he dotes on her, drops kisses on her cheek, and flashes her smiles, he doesn't plan to let her go.

* * *

At dinnertime, Jackson announces he's whipped up some grilled salmon.

Alicia laughs. "Please. As if you can cook."

"I know how to work a barbecue," he says, acting offended.

"You know how to use Grubhub, sweetie."

Lucas claps his friend on the back, stage-whispering, "Confession: I ordered the grilled salmon from an app. And it was Caviar, not Grubhub."

"Hey, can I be a spokesperson for Caviar? That app is sick," Jackson says, his dark eyes twinkling with the possibility.

Lucas side-eyes him. "Dude, you have literally never used it. I do the ordering when you're hungry."

"That is not true. I order when you're not around," Jackson says.

"No. You call and ask *me* to order for you," Lucas corrects him.

"That may be true," Jackson concedes.

"That is completely true."

Vaughn clears his throat. "Um, gotta side with Lucas on this one, man. He ordered you the blueberry salad from Whole Foods on the way back to the house."

I snap my gaze to them. Vaughn was with them on the beach?

"Yeah, but he knows the address," Jackson points out.

"You could memorize it too," Lucas suggests.

"Stop that crazy talk." Jackson smiles sheepishly. "Bring it in. Give me a hug like you love me."

Lucas rolls his eyes as he bro-hugs his buddy. "Go eat your salmon. You know I love you like a brother."

"Like a blueberry salad–ordering brother," Vaughn adds, and I briefly meet Haven's gaze like I can tele-graph *Did we miss something while we were screwing for the not-last time?*

But I can't read anything in her eyes, and there's no time to noodle on what went down on the beach with the blueberry salad because as soon as we sit, Alicia says, "Soooo, this raises an interesting point. What if Caviar wanted Jackson to be a spokesperson?"

So begins another round of "How many hoops will you jump through to make this man your client?"

When we finish the meal, Jackson is staring at me. Studying me. My skin prickles from the intensity.

He sets down his fork. "Do you need a Band-Aid? Some Neosporin?"

I furrow my brow. "No. Why?"

"Because you've got one helluva—oh, shit. Dude." He clasps a hand over his mouth, cackling, then lets go. "You have the mother of all hickeys."

Fuck.

Alicia squeals. "Oh my God. You do. You do. Check it out. It looks like Wisconsin."

I don't hazard a glance at Haven. If I meet her

gaze, I might break. "The dairy state, you say?" I ask Alicia, deadpan.

"Like the dairy state was sucked into a tornado. Also, you did not have that on your neck when you arrived this afternoon," Alicia adds coyly, like a feline playing with her supper.

"Josh Summers. You're a tomcat," Vaughn says, shaking his head in admiration.

I meet Haven's eyes for the briefest of seconds. There are stop signs in them, but that's not necessary. I'd never let on.

I rub my hand over my neck. "This? Nah. I just—" But before I can say *I fell at the pool* or *I tripped on a rock*, I reel those excuses back in. They make me sound like an uncoordinated dumbass. Instead, I lean back in my chair, preen, and sigh contentedly. "What can I say? I took a little stroll when you all were snapping pictures, ran into an old flame, and yada, yada, yada."

"You dog!" Jackson punches my shoulder. "Been here a couple hours and getting some yada, yada, yada. What lucky charm are you carrying?"

"I want all the details," Alicia says, waggling her fingertips.

"Yes, Josh. Tell us everything," Vaughn adds, batting his eyes.

I don't need Jason's podcasts or advice on this subject. Still, I hear his voice in my head, reminding me what I know to be true.

A gentleman doesn't kiss and tell.

"I'm afraid I'm going to have to keep Wisconsin all to myself," I say, and even as the crew tries to pry out of me the story behind the state on my neck and the state *of* my neck, I keep my mouth shut.

After all, I've become quite good at hiding my feelings for Haven.

At least, I think I have.

Somehow, I make it through the rest of the evening without touching her, kissing her, or whispering in her ear.

Without telling her all the things I want.

All the things I need.

They're one and the same.

Her.

And the need hasn't gone away after this afternoon's tryst. It's only grown stronger.

So strong, in fact, that when we mingle on the deck after dinner, drinking beer and wine and chatting about the Hamptons, I'm counting down the minutes till I can excuse myself.

It's unlike me to want to be anyplace else but right where I am—with clients or potential clients.

It's not my style to want to jet.

But it's my style tonight, even when I learn that Jackson and Lucas had simply caught up with Vaughn on the beach as he finished his volleyball game, then walked back with him.

That's all. There was no secret moment between Vaughn and the guys. I can steer this ship home. I can win this client. I know how to do it. It's what I've always done. The field is still wide open, as far as I know.

Part of me wonders if I should stay out here, hanging with them. That's what I'd normally do. Be the last one to close down the proverbial bar, cementing my position as head of the pack, first choice.

And yet, I don't want to hang here.

I say good night, head for bed, and find myself plotting the best strategy to sneak into Haven's room.

But she beats me to it.

JOSH

The ocean breeze wafts through the open window. Moonlight streams in, silhouetting her in the dark as she slides the door to the adjoining bathroom closed then stands against the wall, like she's striking a pose.

It's a pose I can't tear my eyes away from. A vision I don't want to erase.

She wears a pink tank top and cotton shorts as she fidgets with the ends of her hair.

Haven's not a nervous person. Years in the spotlight trained her. But right now, she seems out of her element.

I set down the book I was reading on top of the covers next to me.

A thousand questions form on my tongue. A hundred quips.

Fancy meeting you here.

Need some toothpaste?

Want to share a blanket?

But for a guy who talks all day, who finesses deals with savvy wordsmithing, I'm at a loss to utter anything but "Hey."

"Hey." She nibbles on the corner of her lips then twists her hair again. "I was thinking I would really like to sleep with my hair in a French braid tonight."

Slow and warm, a smile spreads across my face. And that warmth travels farther—down my body, all over my skin.

"Sure. Call it the midnight special. My overnight service."

She laughs. "I'll take your overnight service. No one delivers quite like you."

This is why I called it a night. For this possibility. I'm a thousand times happier that she's here than I'd be if Jackson and Alicia commanded a private audience with me this evening. I don't even care if Vaughn is kicking back with them on the deck.

I don't give a hoot because this is what I want most in the whole damn world.

"Come here," I say softly, patting the bed and the space between my legs.

Quietly, she pads across the floor, gets on my bed, and scoots back, settling between my legs. She shakes out her hair. I thread my hands through her hair, prepping it.

I want to lean my face into the strands, inhale her scent, get drunk on her smell. So I do, bringing my nose to her head and enjoying a long, delicious hit of her.

She laughs lightly. "Does that help you do my hair?"

"I didn't do it because it's helpful," I say as I finger-comb a section of her hair into three pieces.

"Why do you do it?"

"Because I'm addicted to your smell," I say.

"Be careful. I hear you might get hooked," she warns playfully.

As I weave the strands, I say, "Too late. Already there."

Her breath hitches, and she says in the faintest of voices, "Me too."

I grit my teeth, willing myself to focus on the task at hand. Her hair. Not this desire to wrap my arms around her, to flip her over, to kiss her from head to toe.

I'm keenly aware I'm no longer fighting my feelings. I'm not fighting a damn thing with her. This is not Las Vegas. This is not the time we pretended we could barely stand each other.

This is a whole new ball game, and I don't have the rule book. But I don't want it either. I'm making everything up as I go along. Figuring out the new borders and boundaries, and if there even are any.

Quietly I braid, and with every weave, she slides a little closer.

"What do you think of this whole thing? This weekend?" she asks as I gather strands above her ears.

"It's a little weird, but weird is what we signed up for, right?"

"I suppose. You're so sharp with your answers," she says.

"So are you."

"Yeah, I am pretty kick-ass," she says with a grin.

"No doubt." I pause for a moment. "What do you make of Vaughn? He seems so laid-back. How can that be what they want?" This conversation feels good, like how we were when we worked together, assessing opportunities jointly.

"I wouldn't worry about him," she says.

"Why?" I ask curiously.

She glances back at me. "I just wouldn't."

"But why?" I press on.

"I know him. Just trust me on this."

For a split second, I want to ask if there's something between them. But I don't have to ask to know the answer. There isn't anything between them. She's here. She came to find me. So I do the opposite of what I did that night in Vegas. I choose to trust her fully.

"Okay. I do trust you. But you haven't told me what you think of this pitchfest."

"I think a lot of things," she whispers.

"Like what?" I ask, reaching for the hair tie on her wrist.

She lifts her arm, slides it off, and offers it to me. Taking it, I also seize the chance to press a kiss to her wrist.

I'm rewarded with a sweet, sexy sigh.

"Like . . . things are becoming clear," she says.

"What things?"

"Just . . . things."

Laughing, I loop the ends of her hair in the tie.
"Fine. Don't tell me."

"How does my braid look?" she asks, changing the
topic.

"I'd tell you to get up and check in—"

"I don't want to get up."

"Good. Don't go."

"I won't." She leans back against my chest, and I
wrap my arms around her waist. This moment feels as
close to perfection as has ever existed on earth. Haven
Delilah in my arms. I don't care what is happening in
the rest of the house. I don't give a fuck what's going
down beyond these doors. Fact is, I haven't really
cared this whole day, this whole week. She has all of
my attention, all of my interest.

"Josh?" she whispers.

"Yeah?"

I draw her closer, sweeping my lips over her neck,
making her shiver, making *me* shiver.

"Sometimes I think about nights like this." It's
clearly only the beginning of what's on her mind.

I swallow, waiting for her to tell me more.

"I think about you finding me in the dark," she
continues. "About you coming into my home, into my
bed, and finding me."

This confession makes my heart hammer, my
pulse spike. It makes me see paths to brand-new
possibilities. "What would I find if I came into your

room after dark?" I ask as my hands slide under her shirt, my fingers grazing the soft skin of her belly.

She arches against me, her body seeking my touch. "You'd find me like this, wanting you, thinking of you."

I draw a deep breath, letting it fill me, letting it fuel me. Is this real? Or is this a hot, fevered dream? "Haven," I growl. "I'm always finding you in the dark. It's always you. Every night, it's you."

She reaches back, feeling for me. Sliding her fingers through my hair, driving me out of my mind with lust and desire and something so much stronger, so much more.

"That's why it made me crazy when they were joking about your neck." Her hand slides over my throat. She swivels around, gets on her knees, and clasps my face. "I *hated* that lie you told."

"I hated it too," I say, and she seals her mouth to mine, planting a hot, searing kiss on my lips, like she's marking me. She kisses me ferociously, taking what's hers, burning down the forest of my resistance, leaving me with nothing but this inferno of desire.

When she breaks the kiss, I'm wound up, panting, my hands clasped tightly to her hips.

"I hate the thought that someone else could have done this," she says, then dips her face to my neck and traces the outline of Wisconsin with the tip of her tongue.

Her touch is electric, and I'm vibrating with need. "No one else can," I whisper.

She kisses the mark, lets go, and meets my eyes. Her gaze knocks everything loose in my chest. It topples drawers full of emotion, rattling them open. "Why? Tell me why. Why can't anyone else?"

I flip her to her back. "Don't you get it?"

Making quick work of our clothes, I strip off her tank and shorts, then slide off my boxer briefs.

"Get what?" she asks, trembling, parting her legs for me.

I slide inside her as pleasure crashes over me in waves. My reality teeters on the sheer bliss of being inside her. I move then still myself, meeting her dark gaze. At last, I answer her with the raw reality. "You own me, Haven. You totally fucking own me."

She gasps, and it sounds like she's overcome with emotion. Like she can't even talk.

I don't want to talk.

I don't want to do anything but get close to her.

Closer than I've ever been.

I reach for her leg, hitch it up, and move deeper. I rock into her, filling her, fucking her, making love to her.

This time, we are quiet.

We don't talk.

We muffle all our sounds with kisses and swallowed groans. With moans and murmurs. And with contact. Every time her breath hitches, she circles her arms tighter around my waist and grabs me harder.

I do the same, moving in her, taking her, and bringing her to the edge once again.

She parts her lips, and I know she's about to unleash a gorgeous feral moan to the heavens. I know she can't control it, and I love that she's unraveling so beautifully.

But I know, too, that she won't want a soul to know what we're doing. I cover her mouth with my palm, bring my lips to her ear, and whisper, "I got you. Just let go."

She gasps and groans against my hand, writhing beneath me, coming so damn hard I can't hold back any longer either. I bury my face in her neck, swallowing all my sounds, all the words, everything I want to say to her.

But it's not like keeping it quiet is going to change a damn thing.

She has to know I'm so ridiculously in love with her; I can't think about anything else.

That's what this day has made clear.

And that's why, once she's fallen asleep in my arms, I leave.

23

JOSH

Dear Alicia,

Thank you so much for inviting me here for the weekend. You are an incomparable hostess, and I am grateful for your hospitality.

I appreciate you including me in the consideration for Jackson. He's lucky to have someone like you in his corner, someone so tenacious and passionate. He's going to have a long and prosperous career—I mean that in all honesty, and as I said, honesty is a key trait in an agent. He's also a great guy. Every now and then, an agent gets to represent someone who's a genuinely good person.

But that won't be me.

I'm excusing myself from the running for his represen-tation for entirely personal reasons.

And I'll be cheering him on from the sidelines.

. . .

All the best,

   Josh Summers

24

HAVEN

Blinking, I sit up in my ex's bed. It's empty.

I curse him silently for being gone.

But maybe he's in the little boys' room?

I pad across the floor. Nope. No Josh.

Do I want to conduct a furtive search for him on the premises?

I spot a white slip of paper on the pillow, and with nervous fingers, and a trembling heart, I unfold it.

Haven,

Call me sometime. Sometime soon. Like, maybe after you win this client, since I know you'll nab him.

Also, when you call me, I'll tell you why I left. It's not what you think.

I know you want to win fair and square. Trust me, when you do win, you will have won because you deserve it.

Until then, don't take too long to find me in the dark.

Josh

25

JOSH

Dom Pinkerton stomps through the gardens at his house in Greenwich, Connecticut, where I've been summoned.

Summoned at eight in the morning on a Saturday.

When I texted him in the middle of the night and told him I was bowing out, he told me: *Get your ass to Connecticut like you're in the Batmobile.* I gird myself for the biggest dressing down of my career.

His pool-ball head is shiny and pink. He's been sweating as he tends to the orchids, shouting at an orange flower. "Do you know what I hate more than losing a client?"

"No, sir," I say, bracing myself for an epic lashing.

He flaps his arms, pointing to the gardens. "Losing an orchid. Look at these beauties. Look at my babies." He gestures tenderly to a flower with delicate orange petals. "This here is Polly. Polly is a Cattleya Sierra Doll. A hybrid. She's as close to perfection as you'll get with orchids. And right now, I should be talking to Polly, nurturing her, growing her. Instead, what am I doing?"

"Talking to me, sir."

He huffs. "So, why the hell did you think it was a good idea to *recuse* yourself? This is getting to be a habit with you, isn't it?"

I wince but take it on the chin. "Seems it is, sir."

"What's your goddamn reason this time? Is it about a woman again?"

I lick my lips, take a breath, and answer him. "Yes and no."

"It's awfully convenient to hedge your bets like that."

"It's both."

"Get it together, Summers. Last time, you excused yourself from a vote on a promotion because you had"—he stops to draw air quotes—"'feelings for Haven.' Translation: you were in love with her, and I fucking knew it."

I'm speechless for a moment because I didn't think he knew how deep it went. All I'd said was I cared for her. I'd never said we had a thing. I'd never said I was in love. But maybe I didn't have to.

Maybe it was more obvious than I thought.

"I do have it together." I mean it completely. "This was a calculated decision."

"Oh, it was? And how's that?" He crosses his arms.

I take a beat, waiting for regret to wash over me. Nope, the wave doesn't come. I don't regret walking away from a client I didn't court, didn't chase, didn't crave.

That has nothing to do with Jackson and everything to do with me. "Because I didn't want it badly enough."

His jaw ticks. "Information that would have been helpful yesterday, so I could have reminded you of all the reasons you ought to want this. Like this one: because it's your fucking job to want it."

That's the problem. My job ought to be motivation enough. I love my job. Love it to the ends of the earth and back. But I love something else more. And I can't get excited for new work the way I used to. I can't focus the way I used to.

And that's a problem I need to fix. But I couldn't fix it with her in the same room, same house, or the same space as me.

"I understand why you're upset, sir. But here's the issue: I walked away from it because I wasn't invested the way you'd want me to be. My focus was elsewhere, and I don't regret stepping down from contention. Do you regret it when you don't give your orchids all the attention they deserve?"

"Of course," he says with a derisive scoff. "But we're not talking about my orchids."

"But we are, in a way. Likewise, do you regret it when you spend a weekend away from your wife when you could have been with her?"

His eyes narrow, and he lifts his chin. "What are you getting at?"

I sigh deeply. "You want me to regret this decision, but I don't. If you're going to fire me, then fire me." I hold my hands out in surrender, but I feel no sadness. "The fact is, I had to drop out. So I did."

He growls. Literally growls. "What are you going to do next? I mean it. What the hell are you doing next? I count on you to chase new business. I depend on you to win clients. You're my goddamn top agent, and I need your closing skills. But you didn't close this weekend. You kicked open the door and walked the hell out. That can't happen again, Summers."

"You're right. It can't." For the first time, I completely understand negotiation on a personal level. He who's willing to walk away has all the power. I'll walk, and I've never felt that way before.

That's why I need to regroup.

Because no one tells you that when you fall for a woman who turns your heart inside out, you'll turn your world upside down for her. "I need a few days to get things sorted out. I need a break from work."

"No shit you need a break." Then he waves a hand. "Get out of here. If you don't plan on pulling this crap again, you can show up next Monday. If you don't, thanks for all the money you made me. Now leave, so I can talk to Polly."

I catch an Uber into the city and tell Jason he'd better be at the park in an hour because I need his advice.

Badly.

Because I didn't tell Dom the whole story.

My boss doesn't need to know everything. He's never needed to know everything. But I'm finally being honest with myself, and here's the piece I never would have admitted before, the twist I never saw coming.

I *want* her to win.

I *want* her to beat me.

I wanted it the second I heard the end of her conversation with her assistant about Girl Power, and even more when she told me how close she is to the next step in her dreams.

I'm the guy who has an endless capacity in the competitive compartment, and yet the compartment is empty when it comes to her.

Or really, it's full.

Because I want her to have every damn thing she dreams of, and I have to play my part in making that possible.

* * *

We run around the Reservoir.

"I'm having a hard time picturing this," Jason says. "You literally just walked away in the middle of the night? Over a woman, so she could win the deal?"

"Yes," I say as we cruise around the water.

"Yes?" he blurts. "Yes? Yes? Yes?"

"Yes."

"I don't get it. You love your job like you're married to it, yet you didn't care about winning the hottest rising star on the market? Where is my friend Josh, and what did you do with him?"

I shrug as we round a curve. "Didn't care. Not one bit. Still don't. Don't you see? That's the issue, man."

"That's not the *only* issue." Jason can't seem to get past my uncharacteristic forfeit. I get it—I've never walked away from a game, a bet, or a deal I could close. I go balls to the wall on everything. Except last night. "How exactly do you plan on paying those pesky little things known as bills?"

"Dude, I'm not leaving the business. I just left that . . ." I wave a hand in the general direction of the Hamptons. "That scene."

He shoots me an inquisitive stare. "A scene that no longer interested you?"

"Exactly." I slow my pace and heave a sigh. "I didn't want to win the client anymore. I wanted *her* to win. That's the problem—all I can think about is her." I rake a hand through my hair. "All I want is her. She's this constant, persistent presence in my head, in my heart. I can't compete for deals and clients against this woman. I want to hold her and keep her and never let her go. Do you have any idea what that's like?"

He stops and levels me with a stare. "Yes. Yes, I do. Not precisely like that, but I absolutely know what it's like to want someone so much. So I married her, and she's having our baby in a few weeks." He clasps a hand on my shoulder. "But what's your plan? How are you going to navigate work and Haven? Are you just going to drop out of every deal, every race? You vie against her a lot. I'm worried about you, mate. And I never worry about you."

I look up at the sky then back at him, searching for an answer I don't possess. "All I know is I can't work in this in-between state anymore. And I can't be cooped up in a house on the beach where all I want is to be with her but can't. Last night, I had zero interest in the schmooze. And you know me."

He smiles. "You love the schmooze."

"Love it like it's a game-winning homer in the World Series that'll activate a bonus clause. But I didn't want to go mano a mano with her for a client. I can't and I won't, and I'm done with it."

He raises his arms heavenward. "Every now and then, a man achieves complete clarity."

But that's precisely the problem. What do I do with this clarity?

Jason has to take off for an appointment, so I turn to my next set of reinforcements.

* * *

After all, sometimes you need a woman's opinion on the finer details of love.

Fortunately, I have access to a trio of fairer-sex advice-givers, and all three love doling it out freely to their big brother.

I start with Amy, texting to see if she's available to chat. She tells me yes, but she's been saving the world with Quinn, so I'll get two sisters for the price of one.

I find them at a board-game café in the Village that afternoon, huddled over a table in the corner, working to stop the spread of disease in Pandemic. "Have you found the cure yet?"

"Working so damn hard on it," Quinn says then stands and holds out her arms. "Come to the wise ones."

I give her a hug then give Amy the requisite noogie before she tells me she has to use the little girl's room. My youngest sister takes off.

Quinn gestures to the couch. "I hear you need advice. But listen, the key to rescuing humanity is to work together to solve problems, so you can be a medic if you want. I'm a quarantine specialist. And Amy is a researcher," she says handing me a white pawn.

I flop down next to her on the weathered couch and join in the game play, hunting for a cure for four diseases that threaten Earth.

After a few minutes, Quinn looks up from the board, her sage-green eyes twinkling. "So, you're all good?"

I laugh. "Yeah, I just came here to join you in your *let's all hold hands* board game."

"Some things require cooperation, not competition. Also, don't knock Pandemic."

"Pandemic is cool. But I need a little more than game-play advice."

"Ah, you have need of feminine wisdom," Quinn says, like she's a fortune-teller. "Please. Tell me your tale of male dumbassery."

"How do you know I was a dumbass?"

"Gee. Lucky guess?" Quinn flicks her auburn hair off her shoulders; takes a long, thirsty drink of her tea; then makes a rolling gesture with her hand. "Proceed."

"So, there's this woman . . ."

Amy returns, slamming a palm on the wooden table. "Haven!"

"Wait. I know what happened," Quinn adds animatedly, playing up the soothsayer role as she flings her palm to her forehead. "You botched it like only you can?"

I heave a sigh. "I should have requested another audience with Jason for this sort of ribbing."

They both rearrange their features, acting more serious. "Tell us everything you require us to fix," Quinn instructs.

I give them the SparkNotes version of the last few weeks. The PG SparkNotes version. Then I share what I said in the note I left Haven. "So, was that note so bad?"

Quinn answers immediately. "Yes."

"Why? It was . . . *heartfelt*."

"It was half-assed," Quinn corrects. "Don't ask her to come to you. Women don't want that. They want you to go to them and lay it on the line. Seriously. Haven't we trained you better than this?"

"In hair. You trained me in hair."

"And did that do any good?"

I flash back to last night, smiling. "It did some good."

Quinn shoos me in the direction of the door. "Then leave us and go tell her you want to braid her hair for the rest of your life or something."

Sounds about right.

But when I call Haven, she doesn't answer. She's probably still engrossed in pitchapalooza.

When she doesn't respond for a few hours, I go to her place.

Only, she's not there.

Because my doorman calls and tells me there's someone in the lobby waiting for me.

Someone by the name of Haven Delilah.

"Why don't you let her know she's on the list? You can give her the spare key and send her up." Then, with a wry grin, I add, "Tell her I'll be there in twenty minutes, so she won't have much time to rifle through my things."

HAVEN

This calls for a new entry in the rulebook. Rules for what's next.

First, I need to get back to Manhattan stat. I consider a helicopter. Googling the price, I recoil. That's ridic expensive. A car will do just fine.

Along the way, I write down my one new rule.

Find him and tell him everything.

Yes, everything. *That* everything.

JOSH

It doesn't take Sherlock Holmes to deduce she's ticked off.

She stands in my kitchen, arms crossed, tapping her toe. Yet, even in her mad-as-hell mode, she steals my heart.

She seems to do that every day.

"What the hell, Summers?"

"What the hell, what?" I ask, tossing my keys on the entryway table. But I don't move. I stand my ground, since she clearly doesn't want me any closer.

She waves to my apartment. "Why the hell am I on the list?"

"That's what you're starting with? You want to know why you're on the list for my building?"

"Well, I spent twenty minutes snooping and all I found were some towels from Target. There wasn't even a good watch anywhere."

I lift my wrist. "The watch is on me. And Target

has good towels."

"I know. I love Target. Everyone loves Target. Also, the bathroom is nice, and I needed to pee, so thanks for the permission to check everything out. But enough about that." Her jaw is clenched hard, and her folded arms tighten. "Why am I on the list?"

"I put you on it a year ago and never took you off."

"Why?"

A laugh bursts from my chest as I toss her question back at her. "Why do you think?"

She fumes. "Second, why did you . . .?" She stops and waves her arms like a duck flapping away from the water. "Why the hell did you do that at Alicia's house? Just take off like that? This feels like last time all over again. You bowed out."

"Is it the same as last time?" I arch a brow. "Did I *just* bow out? Is that truly what I did? Also, hello? Did you get him?"

She stares icy daggers at me. "You *did* bow out. You excused yourself. Just like you excused yourself from voting on my promotion."

"And that turned out to be the best thing that happened to you. You said that to me."

She huffs. "Don't twist my words, Summers." She's pissed, but not in the way she used to be, where it felt like she was going to claw my eyes out. Her tone is different, but I can't quite place my finger on how it's changed.

"But it did work out," I say gently.

Her shoulders sag, and her voice softens around

the edges. "Josh, I want to win business fair and square. I don't want you to just hand me things because . . ." She stops like she can't bear to say the words.

That's my opening. I close the distance, run a hand down her bare arm, and finish with the truth. "Because I'm in love with you?" I meet her gaze and her brown eyes widen. "Is that what you were going to say? I can't just hand you things because I'm in love with you?"

She nods, her eyes shimmering with something like hope. She's quiet, though, so I keep going.

"There are a number of other ways to finish that sentence too," I say. "Because I've been in love with you this whole time. Because I fell wildly in love with you more than a year ago and I never fell out. Because when I told Dom last year I had feelings for you, that only scratched the surface. Because it's so much more than feelings."

She purses her lips as if she's holding in words that threaten to break free. I brush my thumb across her jaw, and like the cat she is, she rubs her cheek against my palm. "Because *that's* the reason I haven't been with anyone else in the last year, not on a date, not anything. That's why you're on the list for my apartment. I can't think about anyone but you. How could I? You have all of me and have for a long time, Haven."

Then it's her turn, and she sighs, giving me pause for just a second. But only a second, since she loops her arms around my neck. "That's why I'm pissed at you. You always want to go first. You always want to win. And I wanted to win this one. I wanted to tell you first, you big idiot." She yanks me closer, grips me harder. "You drive me crazy because I'm so stupidly in love with you."

My smile grows ten thousand times. My heart expands to the tip of Manhattan and back. I have the answer: her irritation with me is different now because it's chased with something else. With the same damn emotion I feel for her. "Join the club."

"I've been a member for a long time. Every time I see you, it's a fight not to let on."

I lean my head back and laugh. "You are a fantastic actress, then, because you never broke character."

"Oh, please. You couldn't see through the act?"

"The 'I hate you' act?"

She nods, a clever grin on her face. "Yes. I had to fight my feelings for you constantly, or else I'd tell you everything."

I slide my arm around her, grazing my palm down her spine. "And what's everything, snow queen?"

She narrows her eyes. "You know."

I smirk. "Do I? Tell me again, just to make sure I heard right."

She smacks my chest playfully. "I love you. There. Okay?"

Laughing, I drop a kiss to the hollow of her throat. "I like hearing it."

She shrugs away from me, setting her hands on my shoulders. "But what do we do about this? You can't just leave every time if we're trying to win the same thing when it comes to business. You can't bow out. We have to keep going against each other. We're still rivals in business."

I shrug. "I know, but for me it didn't feel right going for Jackson. And it's different than when I recused myself from the promotion vote. Then, I didn't feel I could be fair given how I was secretly falling in love with you. This time, all I could think about was you, and I knew I had to deal with how insanely in love with you I am before I dealt with work. We'll figure out the whole rivals in business thing later. Right now, I don't want to compete with you. I don't want to fight with you."

She wiggles her brows. "What do you want to do?"

I inch closer. "I want to love you." I press a kiss to her soft lips, and she trembles. "Adore you." A kiss to her neck. "Worship you." She shivers. "And fuck you and make love to you." Another kiss. Another shudder. "And most of all," I say, stepping back to meet her gaze, "I want to be with you. In the open. Not in secret. I want you to be mine, Haven Delilah. All mine."

She melts against me. "Don't you know?"

"Know what?"

She lifts her chin like she's offering herself to me. "I am yours. I always have been."

She kisses me, and I see stars, and it's spectacular.

When she breaks the kiss, she says, "Now, do you want me to tell you what happened after you left?"

28

JOSH

I pour her some wine. She picks up the bottle, studying the label. "This is my favorite chardonnay."

"I know. That's why I have it. I bought it this morning."

One brow lifts. "In case I showed up?"

I smile. "And wasn't that wise?" I hand her the glass, and she takes a drink.

"Wise, as in you're a wiseass."

"Speaking of ass." I grab a handful of hers.

She swats me away and heads for the couch as I pour a glass for myself.

As she settles in, she says, "First, Alicia was not happy with you."

"She told you that? That doesn't sound like her."

Haven shakes her head as she sinks onto the plush gray sofa, making herself at home. Damn, she looks great as she relaxes in my living room, sliding so seamlessly into this next phase of *us*.

"No, she didn't tell me, but it was obvious when I found her in the kitchen, huffing and puffing as she brewed coffee."

"Ah, she did that thing people do when they're pissed—they slam cupboards and do everything with a certain angry panache?"

Haven smiles. "She was full of angry panache. But then she got over it and wanted to go for a run, so I joined her."

"Of course you did. And did you bond with her as you ran?"

"We talked about Girl Power, and she was really into the charity. So that was good. When we returned, she excused herself to chat with Jackson and Lucas, so I had another coffee with Vaughn. When she reappeared, she announced that you'd left for personal reasons, but it didn't matter because she'd made her decision already."

She takes a sip, seeming to delight in the wine, then sets down her glass.

She says nothing.

I wait for her to share the good news. "Well, you got it, right?"

I expect her eyes to twinkle with a little spark from the competitive fire that is stoked so easily in her. Instead, she's all vulnerability as she says, "There's something I need to tell you, and I hope you'll understand."

Tension shoots through me. Those are not words you want to hear—not in that combination, not at a time like this. "Okay," I say, steeling myself for whatever's about to blindside me.

She sits up straighter, tucks her legs under her, and takes a breath. Her chocolate eyes blaze with the same intensity I saw in them when she competed, when she launched herself from the top of a mountain and flew through the snow.

"*We* won it."

I narrow my eyes. Her words don't compute. How could she and I have won it?

"What do you mean? You and me?"

She shakes her head. "No. Not you and me, Josh."

"Then who?" I ask just as quickly, then the answer dawns on me. "You and . . . Vaughn?"

She flashes a smile. "Yes, Vaughn and me."

I jerk back. "It went to the two of you? But how?"

"Alicia wanted both of us, and that worked out really well because . . ." She takes a moment to draw another deep breath. "Because Vaughn and I are going into business together."

29

JOSH

That's a curveball I didn't see coming.

"How did that happen? That's an interesting development, to say the least."

She answers quickly, like she's nervous I won't like what she has to say. "We reconnected last week before all this started, just talking about business and how he was leaving Dick's shop."

My brow knits. "He's leaving Dick's firm?"

"He left, Josh. He left a few weeks ago. He wasn't there representing Dick Blaine."

I flash back to the car ride, recalling Vaughn's words when I asked about Dick. *Ever make a decision you regret?*

Then he said he'd spent most of the last year untangling himself from a bad decision.

Holy shit. I break out in a grin. "The dude was there on his own. Damn. I had no idea. That's impressive. I'm psyched to hear that."

"I was too."

"But when did you two make these plans?"

"This morning." Her voice rises.

"After I left and before Alicia made her decision?" I ask, like I need to clarify precisely when "morning" occurs.

"Yes. Like I said, we'd tossed around the idea, and we'd been talking about it as a possibility earlier in the week, but once you were gone, everything was crystal clear. I hope you're not upset, but we work well together. He has a great rapport with clients and gets along with everyone, and he has an analytical mind. We make a great team."

For a flash of a second, the green-eyed monster thrashes in my chest. The caveman that lurks in all of us wants to claim Haven as mine, and only mine. But that's stupid as fuck because she's simply going into business with another guy. She's not going home to that guy. I'm the man she's going to come home to. And now that she lays out their plan, it makes perfect sense. I can picture them as a power tag team.

"Say something. You're upset," she says, worry coloring her tone.

For a second, maybe several, I let myself imagine all the reasons I could be upset.

But nope. I can't find one. "Why would I be upset?"

"Because I didn't tell you till now?"

"You didn't know till today, and I would never expect you to have told me while you were exploring it. And we weren't even officially together till now. I *might* have been jealous for a couple seconds, but then I remembered I'm going to make you scream my name in a few seconds."

She laughs, then breathes a huge sigh of relief. "I'm so glad you said that."

"That I'm going to make you come?"

"Yes, Josh. And the other part too."

I tap her knee. "You're happy about this plan with Vaughn? You like this? You feel good about it?"

"So good," she says with the start of a smile.

I grin wickedly. "Then get over here and take your clothes off, because we should celebrate with your favorite thing."

Coyly, she asks, "What's that?"

"As if you don't know," I say, moving matters along as I move over to her, tug off her top, and pull down her skirt.

"Ohhhhh. You mean . . ." She drops her voice to a whisper. "Orgasms?"

"Yes, woman. Orgasms. You need several to celebrate this awesome, fantastic, amazing win that I couldn't be happier about."

That's the thing. I want her to have everything good in the world. And I want her to have all the pleasure she could want from me.

"And you wonder why I couldn't get you out of my mind for the last year," she says as she yanks off my T-shirt.

"Actually, I never wondered that. I completely understand why you're into me."

She swats my arm. "Cocky bastard."

"Feel free to call me that while my face is between your thighs and you're coming on my lips."

In a few minutes, she's doing just that, her voice hitting that terrific high note, and it's absolutely fantastic. But that's not the best part.

The best part is knowing she's not walking away.

And I'm not either.

Wait.

Let me revise that.

The best part is knowing we'll be together again tomorrow, and the next night, and the one after that too.

That's the biggest win of all.

30

JOSH

In the morning I wake up to a barrage of messages from Jason, Amy, and Quinn.

Jason: Assuming you've acted properly on your clarity, how did it turn out?

Amy: May I now point out a perfect template for your future? Mary Matalin and James Carville. They've pulled off the whole competitors thing. You can too.

Quinn: When can I start planning your wedding?

I laugh quietly as Haven rustles under the covers, shifting onto her stomach, still sound asleep.

I start with Quinn.

Josh: You're a party planner, not a wedding planner.

Quinn: Thanks for raining on my parade. Also, I've planned a few weddings too, oh ye of little faith.

Next, I tackle Jason's note and give him an update. He responds immediately.

Jason: I know you used my advice as inspiration. You can say it—"Jason, you're so damn helpful."

Josh: You're so damn helpful.

Finally, I respond to Amy.

Josh: You had to use the political power couple from another era because there really isn't any other great example of competitor couples, is there?

Amy: True. But also, is there anyone more romantic

in all the world than a pair of political strategists from opposite sides? Besides, I was right.

Josh: You were right about what?

Amy: Darcy and Bennet. *Pride and Prejudice*. I told you so.

Josh: You're right. You're always right.

I set the phone down, look at the sleeping woman by my side, and say out loud, "You were right."

* * *

It's Sunday in Manhattan.

Quickly, we learn that we don't do Sundays in New York the way it's done in the movies. Or on Instagram.

We're not one of those stroll-along-a-quiet-side-street-holding-hands couples.

We don't gather in a line that winds around the block for the new trendy brunch joint.

And we definitely don't do Sunday Funday shit like go ax-throwing after day-drinking. Which, incidentally, sounds like a terrible idea.

Instead, we fuck when she wakes up.

And we shower.

And then we hit the phones.

She has calls to take from Alicia, from Vaughn, and from her other clients.

And I have calls to make too. As Haven paces across the bedroom, I settle into my couch to catch up with my Yankees shortstop, then with my Knicks center, and then with Zane, who texts that he has something to tell me, so I call him right away.

"Dude! Word on the street is sick," he announces.

"Lay the word on me."

"Get this. I hear . . ." He stops, pauses, and seems to draw an excited breath. "Tom Cruise has to skateboard in the next *Mission Impossible* flick."

My brow knits. That sounds unlikely, but then again, everything Cruise does in *Mission Impossible* is the definition of unlikely. "Is that so?"

"Yes! How rad is that?"

"The raddest. Where did you hear that?"

"From Jako," he says, naming his teammate and fellow skater.

"Does Jako have intel about Hollywood flicks?"

"Yes, he has a cousin—well, a second cousin—who works in the biz. You know, does catering and shit for a TV studio in Canada, so he's totally in the know. Wait. Nope. Wrong. He works in Georgia. I get those mixed up a lot."

"Ah, so he's a great source for what's coming down the pike in *Hollywood*."

"Definitely. And listen, here's the thing. Tom's short and all and I'm not, but those are just details. I want to be his skateboarding stunt double. Can you make that happen? I mean, if anyone can make that happen, it's you, right?"

I laugh, even though I'm about to break his heart. "Zane, my man. I hate to be the bearer of bad news, but Tom Cruise does all his own stunts."

Zane groans, an epic sound of sadness that carries across continents and through the halls of time. "No!"

But I can't leave him on that kind of bubble-burst, so I tell him I'm working on renewing his contract with Vans, with a huge increase, and I swear I can see the smile on his face.

"Dude. For that kind of money, I can buy myself a walk-on role in *MI*."

"Aim for the stars, my man. Aim for the stars."

A few minutes later, Haven emerges from the bedroom, looking energized. "Check out this email. We just landed a huge donation from Wu Media to fund the next set of programs I was mentioning. The woman who runs that company is a goddess and so is her director of charitable outreach. Listen to what she wrote."

Dear Haven,

LOVED your terrific presentation. We're thrilled with the fantastic work you're doing at Girl Power. To see the impact of these programs on the lives of young girls who need them is incredibly rewarding on so many levels. Personally, I can vouch for the difference sports made for me -- those early morning practices when I had to rise at the rooster crack of dawn gave me the discipline I needed to succeed not just in sports, but in school.

What more could I ask for! That's why we're so excited to support the work you're doing.

P.S. you were an inspiration to me during your gold medal run. You're fearless and I love it!

My best,
*   Sadie, from Valerie Wu's office*

Haven grins proudly.

"Well done, my fearless, inspiring snow leopard."

"Thank you." She sighs, relieved. "I was really hoping this funding would come through. And I also just had a great call with my new business partner."

"Is that so?"

She wiggles her eyebrows. "So great, in fact, that we are going to kick your ass."

And that's all it takes. My competitive fire is fully stoked once more.

"Woman, I am going to love competing with you and Vaughn and beating the two of you every single day."

She parks her hands on her hips. "Good luck. We're double trouble now."

"Which makes it all the more exciting when I kick unholy ass every day." I get up from the couch, stalk over to her, toss her over my shoulder, and carry her to the bed, where I put her down. "Besides, competing with you gives us a chance to fuck it out every night," I say as I strip off her shirt.

"So it turns you on when I tell you we're going to destroy you?" she asks in the sexiest voice I've ever heard.

I nod. "It absolutely does. Because I'm going to crush you."

Then we do what we've always done best.

We fuck it out.

The next day, I return to work, ready and energized as I walk into the lobby of the skyscraper.

When I reach my floor, Ford and Viviana are waiting outside my office.

31

JOSH

I make a show of checking my watch. "If memory serves, you won't know about a bun in the oven for another week."

Viviana stares at me, her expression unreadable. "I barfed this morning. I wanted to share the news with you first before I head to the lit department meeting."

"Did you? That's awesome," I say, excited for her.

"No, asshole," she says, since Viv always talks to me like one of the guys. "I didn't barf, and I wouldn't expect to barf so early. We still don't know. We'll know soon, but that's not why we're here."

Ford gestures to my office. "Let's chat."

A dart of worry shoots through me, but I try to make light of it. "This sounds mildly ominous."

"Only mildly," Ford echoes as he shuts the door behind me.

I sit at my desk, and they park themselves across from me. "Okay, who died?"

Viviana bats first, concern in her eyes. "Has he contacted you yet?"

"Who?"

Viviana glances at the door and whispers, "Austin."

The hair on the back of my neck stands on end. "No, why? What's going on?"

"I have some friends at the gym where he works out. I rep one of the celeb trainers there who wrote a fitness book."

I sit up ramrod straight. "And?"

"Apparently, there are a handful of women who have worked with him in various capacities. A physical therapist. A nutritionist. Even the team's receptionist."

My gut churns as I realize where this is going. I knew that guy was bad news. "How bad is it?"

Ford cuts in. "He's not the worst. But it seems he has quite a habit of making lewd comments to the women he works with. Suggestive comments." Ford makes a rolling gesture with his hand.

"The kind of comments that suggest a woman should get on her knees and suck his dick if she wants to keep working with him?"

Ford taps his nose and points at me. "Bingo."

I groan, sinking back in my chair. "This is one hell of a Monday morning back at the office." But it seems to be the sign I need.

Viviana offers a sympathetic smile. "Sorry. We wanted you to hear it from us before you heard it from Dom. But the news is starting to get out."

I turn to Ford, recalling our conversation from the other week. "Ford, you know this is when I stop evaluating him on his performance, right? Tell me you know that, man."

"I abso-fucking-lutely know it."

My phone buzzes, and it's Dom's assistant calling me to his office.

* * *

The wheels are turning quickly in my head, picking up locomotive-like speed. I tell her I'll be there shortly, then Ford and Viv leave. Before I go upstairs, I fire off a quick email to Austin.

On the elevator ride to Dom's office, I feel no nerves. I experience zero questions. I have complete clarity about what will happen next, and then what will happen after that.

I open the door as he barks into the phone. "Polly is sick. The fertilizer you gave me is shit. Total shit. And my wife is not happy, and I'm not happy, and no one is happy. Fix this now."

As he shouts more orders, I do something I've never done in his office.

I sit.

When he hangs up, he turns to me. "Listen, glad you're back. I need you now more than ever. You're my rock star, Summers. And we're going to need to finesse the fuck out of this Austin news that's starting to leak. Get a publicist and work on the whole 'innocent until proven guilty' angle."

I say nothing, and Dom stares down at me as if he just realized I was sitting. "What are you doing?" He sounds unnerved.

I smile, so damn certain of where I stand on this front. ON every front. "No."

"Excuse me?"

"No. I won't work on the whole 'innocent until proven guilty' angle."

"Why the fuck not?"

I meet his gaze, certainty my foundation. "Because Austin's an asshole. He's pushing one hundred on the asshole level."

"He's gold on the field, Josh. We're his agents. We need to look out for him."

I shrug, cross my leg, and draw a contented breath. Because I am indeed content about this decision. And I'm content about what will happen next. Everything is coming together in my head. I know where I'm going. I know where my professional future lies. I have the map, and I'm following it. "Nah. I don't think so."

His eyes might pop out of their sockets. I swear they're on springs now. "'I don't think so'?" he repeats like a parrot.

I scratch my jaw, exhale, and nod. "Exactly."

"But that's what we have to do." He points at me. "That's what *you* have to do."

Clarity, it rocks. "And yet, I'm not going to."

"Why the fuck not?"

"Because I'm not repping him anymore."

"Are we doing this again? Where you just bow out because you goddamn feel like it?"

I inhale deeply, that certainty fueling me. "Seems we are."

"No, we're not. You need to work on this."

I laugh, knowing I have an ace in the hole. Maybe Dom's content to let Austin potentially ruin the reputation of the firm with his sorry one, but he's not going to mess with mine. "Let me make myself completely clear. Austin is a misogynistic dick. Case closed. But hey, you can feel free to rep him." I stand.

He points at me, steam rising from the top of his head. "You don't give me your sloppy seconds. That's not how it works here."

"That's cool. Because I don't work here anymore either. I quit." I walk to the door, stopping as I'm about to cross the threshold. "I hope Polly gets better. Here's a tip. Maybe stop yelling. That might help her perk up."

Then I walk the hell out.

32

JOSH

The barista hands me a black coffee. "Just the way you like it."

She slides a lavender matcha latte with caramel something or other to Ford. "And here's your regular."

"Mmm. Smells as delish as ever."

"Or as disgusting," I say as we head to a table in the corner for a meeting. This is exactly what I envisioned when I walked into Dom's office about a week ago. Well, maybe not *this* coffee shop. But *this* next step.

"Don't be knocking my beverage of choice."

"I can't not, Ford. You know that."

We sit, and the guy across from us shouts into his phone, *"Get the chia seeds. I'll Venmo you the money later!"*

I heave a sigh, gesturing to him. "We can't keep meeting like this."

"No shit. We need office space, and we need it stat."

"I've got calls out and another meeting with a realtor later. But what about a name? We need to settle on a name."

Ford takes a drink then sets down the steaming mug. "Alphabetical is the only way to go. Grayson and Summers, my man. Grayson and Summers."

"Summers and Grayson has a particularly nice ring to it."

He shakes his head. "You can't win this one. It has to be Grayson and Summers."

"You're such a hard-ass."

"So are you."

"And I take that as a compliment of the highest order from one of the founding partners of Summers and Grayson."

Ford said sayonara the same day I did, taking off right along with me to start our own shop. Viv's still there, but she's in the lit department, and all is well with her.

I take a drink of the coffee then set it down. "So, tomorrow you find out if you hit the jackpot?"

He nods. "She's taking the test first thing."

"I'm rooting for you guys," I say. "You're not worried, though, about the effort it's going to take to run a new business while starting a family, are you?"

He shrugs. "Nah. I mean, it would be nice if it didn't all fall on the two of us, but that's how it goes."

An idea sparks from out of nowhere and ignites, bright and fiery.

"What if it didn't all fall on the two of us?"

33

HAVEN

We round the corner and head into the restaurant off Park Avenue. Josh called me midmorning and asked if Vaughn and I could meet Ford and him for dinner. *As if* I couldn't figure out what he wanted to talk about.

Vaughn and I are early. Because I know Josh's style. He's always early. "So we have to be earlier," I say to my partner.

"I love it. You have all the intel now on one of our top competitors."

"But listen—we don't want it to seem like we had the exact same idea."

Vaughn flashes an easy grin. That's what I like about him. He's easy to get along with, easy to do business with, and still tough as nails when it comes to negotiating.

"Don't worry, Goldie," he says, using his nickname for me, since he has a thing for nicknames. "I'm the master at making it seem like anything is someone else's great idea. Like the time I mentioned how much fun volleyball on the beach was, and I knew that would lure Lucas and Jackson to swing by."

I shake my head appreciatively. "Have I mentioned how much I like your sneaky, devilish side?"

"I believe you have. Many times."

We grab a table at the swank sushi place that my boyfriend loves—it's still strange to call Josh my boyfriend, but it's completely wonderful too. Vaughn and I order wine and chat about how our new firm is going.

A few minutes later, Josh strides in, looking sexy as sin in a suit and tie, like he always does. I drop a kiss to his cheek, then say hi to Ford, who's by his side.

"Looking lovely, Haven," Ford says.

"And you're as sharp as ever."

Ford claps a hand to Vaughn's shoulder. "Good to see you again, bro. So stoked you left Dick Blaine. But how the hell were you there in the first place?"

Vaughn shrugs and smiles. "What can I say? There was this girl I was seeing at the time, and she convinced me I'd make more money there, and I'd need more money if I was going to want to be with her, and so on."

"Ouch. I trust you're not with Miss Monopoly anymore?"

"She's long gone."

"Anyone new on the horizon?" Ford asks.

Josh shoots him a look. "What? Are you a matchmaker now? You going to set him up with Viv's sister?"

Ford's eyes widen. "Not a bad idea. But I was thinking how about one of your sisters?"

I nudge Vaughn's elbow. "Let's see. Amy, Tabitha, or Quinn? I'm trying to picture—"

"Hey now. Can we leave my sisters out of this?" Josh laughs, takes a seat, and steers the conversation exactly where I expected him to. "Lady . . . and gentlemen, let's cut to the chase. How does Delilah, Channing, Grayson, and Summers sound to you?"

I beam privately. I had a hunch. A damn good one, and this is exactly what I wanted as well. What *we* wanted. But I know a thing or two about negotiation, so I maintain my game face like I'm staring down a double black diamond run in the Olympics. "I hadn't thought of that before."

"Yeah, me neither. What makes you guys want to do that?" Vaughn asks.

Josh leans forward, an intense look in his dark eyes. "Listen, you two bring something special to the table. You're former athletes and you're sharp as nails. You're fierce and loyal and devoted. You think outside the box. And the two of us," Josh says, pointing from Ford to himself, "we know contracts. We know deals. We find loopholes and exploit them. The four of us would be unstoppable."

"A powerhouse," Ford adds.

Vaughn leans back in his chair and strokes his chin. "Sort of like an all-star team, you're saying?"

"The 1927 Yankees," Josh adds, since the man loves his baseball metaphors.

"The fab four," Ford adds.

Vaughn turns to me, his bluff in full force. "That's an interesting idea. Huh. What do you think, Haven? Lady and the champs?"

I take a drink of my wine and glance at the ceiling like I'm considering this partnership for the first time. I turn to the guys across from us. "Tell us more."

Josh and Ford share more of their vision, and it's everything we could want. It's the perfect match. When they're done, I look at my business partner again, shrugging nonchalantly. "It's not a bad idea."

"Not a bad idea at all."

"Especially since you put my last name first. Delilah."

Ford jumps in. "Hey! She's not first alphabetically. Vaughn's is as in Vaughn Channing."

Josh smacks his arm. "Dude, ladies first. Don't you know that?"

Later that night, I spill everything to Josh. "I wanted the same thing. To work with you two. I just wanted you to think you were first."

"You're so clever. Always working the angles. Negotiating till the end. Should I make you negotiate for orgasms?" He crawls over me on the bed, caging me in with his arms.

"You would never make me wheel and deal for Os."

"And why's that?"

I loop my arms around his neck. "Because you love giving them to me."

He drops his mouth to my neck, pressing a hot kiss to my skin. "What can I say? All my cards are on the table with you."

"And I like it that way," I say, squirming as he blazes a trail of kisses up to my ear.

He breaks the kiss. "Like it?"

I grab his chin. "Love it. Like I love you. Madly."

"And for that, you deserve your favorite thing."

"Sounds like I won," I whisper.

But then, I'm winning at everything with the man I love. The man I missed. The man I'm so damn glad is mine again.

For now, and for always.

34

FORD

The next morning, I'm awake before the sun. I'm up before the goddamn birds. Hell, I barely slept a wink all night.

In the last few days, I've offered up ten thousand prayers to the universe, and thrown all my coins in all the fountains in the city. Last night I wished upon a star.

Again.

I made the same damn wish I've made every time I've seen a star during the last several months.

You hear about friends who send the puck screaming into the goal on the first shot. And that makes you think it'll be that way for you.

It hasn't been that way for us.

It's been eight months, and don't get me wrong, the last eight months have been fantastic. We've enjoyed the kitchen counter, the washing machine (Viv digs the assistance the spin cycle offers), the dryer, the dining room table (Don't worry, future Thanksgiving guests, we cleaned up), the couch, the staircase (That shit hurts and my back was a mess for days), as well as the shower (Why doesn't anyone tell you that up-against-the-wall shower nookie should be an Olympic event? And if you make it to the end everyone gets a gold medal), and, of course, the bed.

And if we have to try another month and another one too, I will give it my best every damn time.

But I want a baby, and so does Viviana. And I want to give my gorgeous, brilliant, sexy wife everything she wants.

I arrange the pregnancy test on the bathroom counter just so.

I tiptoe downstairs and check on the cupcake I ordered in case it's the news we want.

I let the dog out. I let the dog back in. I go upstairs.

When Viv stretches, yawns, and her eyes flutter open, I flash her a smile. "Good morning, beautiful."

"Good morning, hot stuff."

She takes a long breath, then swings her feet out of bed. She pads to the bathroom and takes her time brushing her teeth.

When she spits out her toothpaste, I tap my toe. "Woman, are you trying to torture me?"

"I don't want to have morning breath if I kiss you when it's positive."

My eyebrows shoot up. "One, I do not care if you have morning breath. Two, don't jinx us."

She shrugs and smiles. "I have a good feeling."

I grab her arm, desperate to know if she knows something. "Why? Did you take one last night?" I shoot her a stern stare. "You better not have found out before me. You will definitely get spanked then."

"Again, not a punishment." She wiggles her hips and juts out her breasts. "I just have a feeling. The girls are a little more . . . sensitive."

I groan appreciatively then dart out my hands. "Let me check that sensitivity for you."

"In a minute!" She shuts the bathroom door, pees, then opens it and holds the stick. The longest two minutes of my life pass . . . till two pink lines appear.

It's the most beautiful sight I've ever seen in my life, and my heart soars.

"In nine months, you'll be a dad! Now kiss me because I don't have morning breath."

"And I don't care if you do, Mama," I say, lifting her up in my arms and crushing my lips to hers.

I've been kissing this woman for the last five years —through dating and engagement and marriage. But this kiss? This searing, fierce kiss that's passionate and tender? It's my new favorite kiss with my wife.

It goes to my head. It goes to my heart. It makes me fall in love with her all over again.

I have a feeling I'll be doing this every damn day for the next nine months, and then long past that into our future, as baby makes three.

I get down on my knees and press a kiss to her belly. She sighs happily and runs her hands through my hair.

I lean my ear against her stomach and say, "Ah, he just kicked for me."

Laughing, she playfully pushes me away, saying, "Maybe it's a girl."

I rise, drop a gentle kiss to her forehead, then whisper, "Want to go for twins?"

"I don't think it works that way, baby. But yes, let's celebrate."

And we do, and it's as good as the night we had home-field advantage a few weeks ago.

Wait. It's even better.

Especially since we share the cupcake when we're through.

35

VAUGHN

A little later

Look, I'm all for ladies first, but that name was a mouthful. We changed it, and now we're rocking hard as The Premiere Agency, landing marquee athletes left and right and bringing the old faithfuls over from our prior shops. All-star indeed.

We rep Jackson Pierce, who is killing it this summer on the court, so Alicia thinks we're all *the best*, as she tells us nearly every day, especially since we inked Jackson a deal as a spokesperson for Caviar. Josh brought over Zane, half the Yankees, and a ton of other major leaguers, while Ford handles a bunch of top football players. Plus, most of my client list from hockey, football, basketball, baseball, and golf joined Premiere. And Haven already had her list of stars.

This gig is epic, and it's so much better than the

prior agency I worked for. I shudder thinking of the last year, when I made some choices I shouldn't have. But hey, every man has a dark moment in his past.

I've put it behind me, and I've moved on.

But I've made one rule now that I'm on the other side of that bad decision: no romantic entanglements. After the way the last gal messed with my heart, I'm wary of dating and I'm suspicious of love.

And that's fine, because I have a business to grow, and I have every intention of doing that and *only that* for the foreseeable future.

Like right now, as I finish a call with the forward for the Rangers. "Feel free to book that trip to Greece with the missus. The deal is done," I say, then congratulate him once more before I end the call.

I look up to see Josh in my doorway. "Epic work on that deal. You ready for our dinner meeting?" he asks.

"Absolutely."

We take off for a nearby restaurant to meet his sister. Quinn's a party planner, and Josh and Haven want to host a holiday party for our clients, and we need to start planning since November is already here.

Josh claps me on the back as we reach the eatery. "Now listen, you shouldn't believe a thing Quinn tells you about me."

"Don't worry. I have sisters. I know how they love to throw brothers under the bus."

"I love them madly, but they're also excellent at blaming me for literally everything."

Inside the restaurant, a woman with flaming red hair waves from the table in the back.

I groan privately.

Why does she have to be a redhead?

Redheads are my weakness. Especially smart, fun, witty, and flirty redheads.

Maybe she'll be dull, banal, and boring.

After a quick intro, Josh excuses himself for the restroom, and I extend a hand to the woman in question. "Good to finally meet you, Quinn. I hear your parties are the stuff of legend."

"And I hear you're the easygoing one in the group."

I take the seat across from her. "Well, you know what they say—don't believe everything you hear."

"Ah, so you're actually tightly wound, cross, and a total ogre," she says with a playful glint in her green eyes.

"Absolutely. I'm the worst," I say with a wink.

"I'll do my best not to upset the dragon in you, then, when we practice ornament decorating and hot-cocoa tasting."

I add witty and fun to the checklist. "Wait. Did you just say hot-cocoa tasting?"

"Does that tickle your fancy?"

"No. It sounds awful, horrible, terrible." I lower my voice to a conspiratorial whisper. "How's that for ogreish?"

She leans a little closer. "You can't fool me. I can

see right through you, and I bet you *love* hot-cocoa tasting."

I quirk a brow. "Is that so?"

She smiles like she has a secret. "It's obvious."

"And how is it obvious?"

She screws up the corner of her lips, studies me, then issues a verdict. "You look like a man who enjoys sweet things."

Smart and flirty, check. And that's it. I'm screwed.

I'm officially screwed, and I'm blaming Josh.

I'm throwing him under the bus for having a sister who's funny, sexy, and clever, and who loves hot chocolate.

But I'll just stay far, far away from her. I'm off the market, and even if I wasn't, I know better than to tango with my new business partner's sister.

Even though dinner with her is fantastic and we get along so well it should be illegal.

At the end of the meal, Josh turns to me. "I need to head out of town for a week. Any chance you can handle the party stuff? Besides, you're way better at it than I am."

"Sure," I say, and when I look at Quinn, I'm not sure if the parties will be the stuff of legend.

But I already know I'll need a legendary amount of willpower to resist her.

EPILOGUE

Josh

A little later

There's a first time for everything.

Today, it's for this brand-new T-shirt at Wimbledon.

I had the shirt custom-made on Zazzle. Haven picked the colors. She insisted.

And boy, did she ever go all out.

She picked pink.

Sparkly pink.

With glitter on top.

We enter the stadium and make our way to the best courtside seats, where Alicia practically tackles us. She's vibrating with jitters.

"You're here! I'm so nervous I've had ten Diet Cokes. But I can't tell Jackson, so I'm telling you." She flaps her hands like she's going to shake out all those butterflies.

"Our boy is going to be great," I reassure her.

"He's the best," Haven seconds. "And no more Diet Cokes for you."

"You're right. Cut me off. Don't let me have any more. Also, you guys are the absolute best! Okay, I need to go take some pics."

She darts off, and I take my seat courtside to watch Jackson play.

I sit up straight as a ruler next to my woman so the slogan on my shirt is completely visible.

Perhaps Haven thinks she got my goat. But the words are all true. *Haven Delilah is the top sports agent in the country.*

And I wear them proudly, making good on our bet.

"This is it. This is officially the hottest you've ever looked," she says as she runs a hand down my arm.

"Hotter than the night I wore the suit you practically ripped off me?"

She shoots me a confused look. "Which do you mean? That sounds like every night."

I laugh. "Hotter than the time I went snowboarding with you and you mauled me on the chairlift because you thought I looked hot in a winter jacket?"

"Snow babes are sexy to me. So sue me."

"Yes, my snow queen." I wiggle my eyebrows. "And

hotter than the time I got down on my knee at Wimbledon and proposed to you?"

She gasps. Clasps a hand to her lips.

I've done it. I've shocked her. And I will cherish the look on her face right now—her wide eyes, the way they shimmer, the utter joy etched in her features.

I flip open the blue velvet box I've pulled from my pocket, and speak from the center of my heart, the core of my soul. "Once upon a time, there was a man and a woman who hated each other. They couldn't stand each other whatsoever. Every time they ran into each other, they brandished their claws. But in the end, all they had to do was talk it out to realize hate was just another four-letter word for love." I take a beat, swallow, and continue. "Haven, I want to find you in the dark every night. I want to find you in the light every day. You own my heart and my head, and you have since I met you. I never want to let you get away. Marry me."

As a tear streaks down her cheek, she nods over and over, choking out her "*Yes.*" Then she pulls me up, tugs me close, and kisses the hell out of me before the tennis match begins.

When she breaks the kiss, I slide the ring on her finger.

She stares at the diamond solitaire, her smile stretching across the ocean. "It's beautiful. I love it so much. I love you so much."

"Good. Let's keep it that way, partner."

She smiles again. "Partner."

We take our seats, and watch our client crush the competition.

* * *

"We brought him good luck with our shirts, don't you think?" I ask when the match ends in a fantastic victory.

She plucks at hers. "I do look good in your college jersey."

Number eighty-eight looks sexy as hell on her. She didn't have to wear it, since technically she won the bet for the rising star. But she said she wanted to, that she'd gladly wear her man's number.

I play with the hem of the football jersey. "This is the sexiest you've ever looked."

She pretends to be aghast. "Hotter than the night you slipped into my room in the Hamptons?"

"You were beautiful then."

"And what about the night I showed up at your place to tell you I loved you?"

"You were a stunning vision that time."

"And even so, this is your favorite?"

"Yes, *Mrs. Summers.* This is now my favorite, since you said yes to me."

She leans her shoulder against mine, grinning. "Once upon a time, a guy thought he hated a girl, but the girl knew better. She knew he'd eventually become her husband."

"There you go. You're always right."

"I am."

* * *

We make our way out of the arena, bumping into Lily, the sports reporter, on the way. She's walking next to a guy who has his hand on the small of her back. "Hey, Lily!" Haven says. "Long time no see."

The reporter whips her head around and flashes a smile. "Hey! Good to see you again. This is my husband, Finn Nichols."

She introduces us to the guy, and we all shake hands.

"Pleasure to meet you all. I heard you were in our hometown earlier this year, and you set the conference on fire."

"Sparks were indeed flying," Haven says, then whispers, "Onstage and off." She waggles her ring. "And look what happened."

"Congratulations," Finn says. "Glad to see the sparks turned into the good kind of fire."

"Let me see that beauty," Lily says, then oohs and ahhs over Haven's ring before she meets my fiancée's eyes. "And now you should ask him to give you an extra special engagement gift.'"

"Oh, should I?" Haven's eyebrows rise, her tone playful.

"Yes. Just ask him for your deepest fantasy," Lily says with a wink.

Finn chuckles. "And I'm sure he'll give it to you."

I lift my chin. "Is that what you did for your woman?"

"Hell, yeah," he says, then drapes a possessive arm around Lily.

I flash back to Haven's comments to Lily after the panel— *You go, girl.*

When Finn and Lily leave, I ask Haven what the gift was all about.

"Oh, just a little present her guy gave her."

"Yeah, I figured that much. Her fantasy and all that. What's the story?"

"I can't tell you her secrets. But suffice to say, she wanted a particular thing, and he gave it to her."

I wrap an arm around my fiancée. "As a good fiancé should do."

ANOTHER EPILOGUE

Haven

A few months later

Time for another show of hands. Is sleeping with the enemy who you're really, truly, completely, madly in love with a bad idea?

I had no idea if Josh felt the same way about me as I did about him back when we were competing for the next big thing. Part of me was sure it was just sex and only sex, and that I was risking my whole damn heart when we fell into bed again and again.

But it turned out sleeping with the enemy was the very thing that helped me let down my guard. Only then was I able to see how he really felt, and to share at last how I felt too.

And that's a damn good thing.

Because the man who was my sworn foe has come

all the way around to the other side. He's my colleague, my life partner, and my big love.

But hate sex is indeed awesome.

And we still have it.

Because we like to role-play.

Sometimes we pretend we're still competitors.

Now and then, we make believe we're enemies.

And other times, we act like we can't stand each other. Mostly when he deliberately messes up a French twist or a braid.

That's when I fume.

And that's when he narrows his eyes at me.

Then we lunge at each other.

Those games don't just turn us on. They bring us closer. And even though we're playing games, we can only do it because we both completely trust each other.

And I do trust him. I trust him with my whole damn heart.

Because he's earned it, because he cherishes it, and because he laid his on the line for me.

With him, I'd say I've won gold, and it's better this time around.

THE END

Read Lily's story in the red-hot erotic novella THE ENGAGEMENT GIFT, available now. Vaughn and Quinn's romance unfolds in the romantic comedy novella SPECIAL DELIVERY. And look forward to

Amy's romance in the romantic comedy ASKING FOR A FRIEND! Be sure to sign up for my newsletter to receive an alert when sexy new books release!

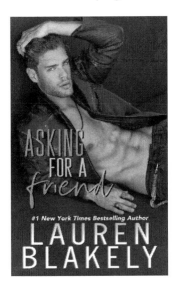

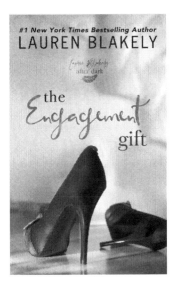

ACKNOWLEDGMENTS

Big thanks to Lauren Clarke, Jen McCoy, Helen Williams, Kim Bias, Virginia, Lynn, Karen, Tiffany, Janice, Stephanie and more for their eyes. Goddess love to Helen for the beautiful cover. Thank you to Kelley and Candi and KP. Massive smooches to Laurelin Paige for access to her brain and heart. As always, my readers make everything possible.

ALSO BY LAUREN BLAKELY

FULL PACKAGE, the #1 New York Times Bestselling romantic comedy!

BIG ROCK, the hit New York Times Bestselling standalone romantic comedy!

MISTER O, also a New York Times Bestselling standalone romantic comedy!

WELL HUNG, a New York Times Bestselling standalone romantic comedy!

JOY RIDE, a USA Today Bestselling standalone romantic comedy!

HARD WOOD, a USA Today Bestselling standalone romantic comedy!

THE SEXY ONE, a New York Times Bestselling standalone romance!

THE HOT ONE, a USA Today Bestselling bestselling standalone romance!

THE KNOCKED UP PLAN, a multi-week USA Today and Amazon Charts Bestselling standalone romance!

MOST VALUABLE PLAYBOY, a sexy multi-week USA

Today Bestselling sports romance! And its companion sports romance, MOST LIKELY TO SCORE!

THE V CARD, a USA Today Bestselling sinfully sexy romantic comedy!

WANDERLUST, a USA Today Bestselling contemporary romance!

COME AS YOU ARE, a Wall Street Journal and multi-week USA Today Bestselling contemporary romance!

PART-TIME LOVER, a multi-week USA Today Bestselling contemporary romance!

UNBREAK MY HEART, an emotional second chance USA Today Bestselling contemporary romance!

BEST LAID PLANS, a sexy friends-to-lovers USA Today Bestselling romance!

The Heartbreakers! The USA Today and WSJ Bestselling rock star series of standalone!

The New York Times and USA Today
Bestselling Seductive Nights series including
Night After Night, After This Night,
and *One More Night*

And the two standalone
romance novels in the Joy Delivered Duet, *Nights With Him*

and Forbidden Nights, both New York Times and USA Today Bestsellers!

Sweet Sinful Nights, Sinful Desire, Sinful Longing and Sinful Love, the complete New York Times Bestselling high-heat romantic suspense series that spins off from Seductive Nights!

Playing With Her Heart, a

USA Today bestseller, and a sexy Seductive Nights spin-off standalone! (Davis and Jill's romance)

21 Stolen Kisses, the USA Today Bestselling forbidden new adult romance!

Caught Up In Us, a New York Times and

USA Today Bestseller! (Kat and Bryan's romance!)

Pretending He's Mine, a Barnes & Noble and

iBooks Bestseller! (Reeve & Sutton's romance)

My USA Today bestselling

No Regrets series that includes

The Thrill of It

(Meet Harley and Trey)

and its sequel

Every Second With You

My New York Times and USA Today

Bestselling Fighting Fire series that includes

Burn For Me

(Smith and Jamie's romance!)

Melt for Him

(Megan and Becker's romance!)

and *Consumed by You*

(Travis and Cara's romance!)

The Sapphire Affair series...

The Sapphire Affair

The Sapphire Heist

Out of Bounds

A New York Times Bestselling sexy sports romance

The Only One

A second chance love story!

Stud Finder

A sexy, flirty romance!

CONTACT

I love hearing from readers! You can find me on Twitter at LaurenBlakely3, Instagram at LaurenBlakelyBooks, Facebook at LaurenBlakelyBooks, or online at LaurenBlakely.com. You can also email me at laurenblakelybooks@gmail.com

Printed by Amazon Italia Logistica S.r.l.
Torrazza Piemonte (TO), Italy